THE VANISHING CAFÉ

HANA ESSELINK

First published in the United Kingdom in December 2017
by Crux Publishing Ltd.

ISBN: 978-1-909979-54-3

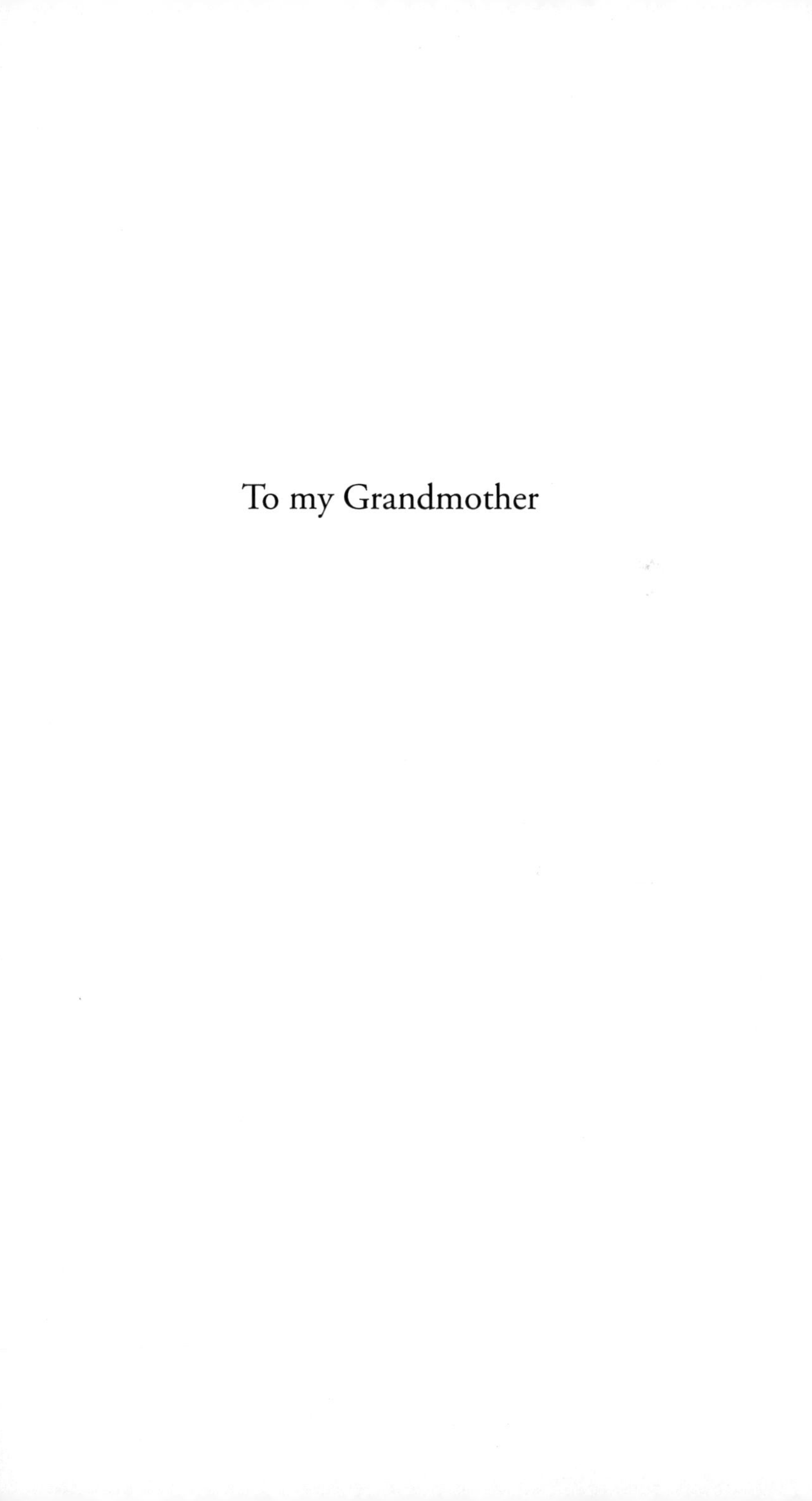

To my Grandmother

"The greatest hazard of all, losing the Self, can occur very quietly in the world, as if it were nothing at all. No other loss can occur so quietly, any other loss – an arm, a leg, five dollars, a wife etc. – is sure to be noticed."

– SOREN KIERKEGAARD,
The Sickness unto Death

"We are like butterflies who flutter for a day and think it is forever."

– CARL SAGAN

CONTENTS

CHAPTER ONE

My grandmother always told me that every person in the world has a story to tell. She said that the next time I walked past someone on the street, I should look closely at them. She told me to look at their eyes, their hands, their posture, and the way in which they carried themselves along their path. Did they betray their persona in these small details? She told me that the life of the ordinary man always contained something unique, sorrowful, twisted and even beautiful in its midst. It was life, she maintained, that bore the troubles of man under its magnificent wing like a mighty bird, it was life that carried all the emotions along its fiery river, it was life that we shaped to give us meaning, and it was life that took all meaning away from us. She said that it was all a question of interpretation, a riddle whose answer was never clear.

Nan, as I affectionately called her, is dead now. She died about five and a half years ago, but her words still remain in my mind, sharp as a flint.

I thought about what she told me on this warm July

day, as I took Pieter, my husband, with me to the café. I had told him a few things about the café over the past five years, all the time that I'd been living in Amsterdam with him. My work for an international charity had kept me busy during that time and I had travelled to other places – Zimbabwe, Kenya, India and Bangladesh, sometimes with Pieter, mostly alone. But we had never come back to London. My work didn't allow me much time off, and when it did, I had visited several other European cities.

Now as I approached the café itself, through the streets of Soho, I felt my anticipation begin to rise. A shiver overcame me, unusual for such a warm day. We walked towards Soho Square. I was nervous about the visit and I wondered who would be sitting there when I entered; would I recognise any of the faces of the people I used to know?

'Darling, tell me why this café is so important to you again,' Pieter said, grabbing my arm to catch up with me.

I turned to face him and people wove their way around us as we stood there.

'It was the place where I evolved spiritually. Where I realised that everything my nan had taught me over the years was in me, like a tree waiting to grow. The experience of this café was more valuable than any treasure.'

'Why Nina? You've never told me this in so much detail before.'

'Well, we're very close to it now and it's all coming back to me. It's just that my nan's words are becoming clear to me and I realise that I came to understand God, as much as anyone can.'

'So, you were born again?' Pieter laughed.

'No, not like the Christian way, but definitely in another way, yes. You see, it was like I'd been in a slumber for years and finally I woke up and saw the reality.'

'All from the café?' He sounded doubtful.

'Yes and the regulars who went there.'

Old Compton Street was busy. The heat had attracted big crowds. People sat outside places I'd never seen before, a new bar had opened and young men in faded jeans and coloured t-shirts, stood on the streets drinking and laughing. Some had fit bodies, tanned, muscular arms, open necked shirts and pierced earrings. There were a number of stylish women dressed in short skirts and heels or flowery dresses, the men chatted together in their groups as tourists passed through with bright coloured rucksacks. A new noodle bar was brimming with people, the smell of fried food drifted out as we walked past. Next to it was a sign indicating that a new patisserie would be opening shortly. A man dressed as a purple cake stood outside handing out leaflets for it.

There was a Lebanese restaurant along the way that was busy. Couples sat on the colourful mosaic style tables outside, dipping pitta bread into hummus and drinking white wine. A live band was playing in a bar further down and the music spilled out into the street.

'It's been a long time since I've been around here,' Pieter said, as two men in smart suits rushed past with their briefcases, laughing loudly. 'Aren't they in the wrong part of town? Shouldn't they be in the city?'

Pieter worked for several international banks and sometimes had to travel to London for business at short notice.

I knew exactly where to find the café, which was just as well because it didn't have a name. Whenever I'd mentioned it to Pieter I'd always called it the café with no name. I remembered that it had a red canopy with a small Brazilian flag woven on the left hand side. Today I looked for that flag as I wove my way through the people.

The café was on Greek Street, off Old Compton Street. I remembered it now. The familiarity of the location came back to me. But as I scanned the street, I found I couldn't locate the canopy. I was puzzled, wondering if I might be mistaken somehow, when suddenly I saw it.

My enthusiasm left me because it appeared desolate. I left Pieter trailing behind me as I walked up to it. It was the same place; but it was shut. There was a For Sale sign hanging in the window. I peered in; the place was deserted and dark, unfriendly and silent.

I turned to face Pieter, and my face must have displayed my dismay, because he smiled at me sympathetically.

'Are you sure this is it?' he asked. I nodded, feeling unsettled.

'This is it,' I said. I looked around, a new bar had opened directly opposite; everything else in the street was achingly familiar. The café looked abandoned in comparison to the busy bar next door. A group of Japanese tourists came out talking loudly and walked past us.

I peered through the glass door, my face pressed up close, searching for a clue as to why it had shut down. The counter facing me was bare. The full-length mirrors were still there on the walls, but the stool and tables were gone, leaving an empty floor. The bookshelves were empty and there wasn't a cup or spoon in sight. The place appeared despondent. I went to the bar next door and asked the owner if he knew what had happened. He told me that the place had been empty for almost six months now, and then he shrugged and said that he didn't know anything else.

I stepped off the pavement's edge and looked at the café. A couple walked past and their reflections lit up the glass briefly. Pieter looked closely at the For Sale sign.

'That place was a living, breathing entity,' I said. There was no sign of the people who were once here. Their voices were as silent and as dead as the café. I didn't know what else to do as I had no way of contacting any of those people. I only felt desperation inside.

'Let's get a drink,' Pieter said, his slight Dutch accent clearly distinguishable. Reluctantly, I let him take my hand and we crossed the road. We sat at one of the tables arranged outside on the street and waited to be served.

'It has been five years.' Pieter said, as if that explained everything.

'It only closed down six months ago,' I said, sadly. 'I should have come to London sooner.'

I stared across at the café and from where I sat it was impossible to see anything more. The secrets from the past lay dead inside the place, hidden forever. The café was now only a graveyard of whisperings and happenings; events trapped inside the silent grey walls; behind the full-length mirrors. The people were gone, it was as if nothing had ever happened. The anticipation had been so great and now it was washed away with disappointment.

'Nina, you've told me only a few things about this place,' Pieter said, his azure blue eyes gazing at me. He smiled and his face lit up, accentuating the soft lines around his mouth. He had a Mediterranean look about him, somewhat uncharacteristic of the Dutch. 'You should have explained it all to me a lot earlier, now you look so sad. What happened here that changed you so much?'

And I told him. It was not just small incidents that I recalled; it was the whole experience. It didn't matter anymore whether it all sounded far-fetched or extraordinary. We sat there, the whole afternoon, drinking coffee and talking.

There was so much that I needed to tell him. Every time I looked at the café, I fancied that it was coming to life again. As Pieter sipped his coffee, I was back in the café again.

***

Time stood still and I saw him again – the very person who I had wanted to see today if only the café had been open. James. That was his name. How could I forget? I saw him in my mind, sitting as he used to in the café, looking through the notes he had prepared for his philosophy seminar. His grey hair was brushed neatly and his glasses were almost slipping off his nose. I saw his hands so clearly that I could have sworn he was there, sipping his tea right in front of me, pushing his glasses back and looking at me, his blue eyes piercing mine, as Pieter's did now.

In my mind, I saw James smile and put his cup down. He affectionately patted my hand.

***

'Are you okay?' Pieter asked, as he reached for my hand and clasped it gently. Pieter finished his coffee and placed the cup back on the table. The waitress asked us if we wanted something else and we said no. She walked back inside the bar and as I watched her, I remembered the café vividly again. The hustle and bustle of people laughing and talking, coming in and out of the place with their food and drink. I saw it just as it had looked five years ago.

I saw the door was wide open, as it used to be during the warmer days, with three tables with a few chairs next to them outside. And I saw the people who opened themselves up when they came to the café, who made it the living entity that it was. Their voices became clear and the faces that belonged to the voices came into focus sharply. The clothes that those people had worn, their mannerisms, the essence of their lives, it was all coming back to me now.

I began to tell Pieter why that summer had meant so much to me, and why the café had been the place where it had all begun. And I began with Davla.

'So, what was she like?' Pieter asked me, smiling.

'She wasn't a babe exactly,' I laughed. 'She just had a way about her.'

'Really? This place doesn't look like all that,' Pieter said. 'I was expecting something a little more…grand.'

I suddenly wondered if I could ever explain to Pieter what the place had fully meant to me. His scepticism was becoming apparent.

'It's not about the size,' I said. 'It was more about the people who came here. Davla – well, she was a mix of fire and ice. The thing about it was, sometimes she was both at the same time.'

I started to tell Pieter the story. The whole story.

CHAPTER TWO

Davla came out of the small café in Greek Street so fast, that she almost knocked me over.

She had just lit a cigarette and I got a good whiff of the smoke as she grabbed my shoulder and apologised. Silver bangles jangled softly together on her arm and her hands looked dry, the chipped red nail polish in need of touching up. Her strong Portuguese accent struck me even though her English was perfect. As she smiled, her green eyes lit up.

'I'm so sorry,' she repeated, waving her arm in the air, her cheeks flushed. She puffed on the cigarette hastily as if she were running out of time, then she threw it away and stubbed it out with the long heel of one of her red sandals.

Her cut off jeans were slung low over her skinny hips and her white top was embroidered with large red flowers.

In the scorching heat, I had almost walked past the café. She hastily took off her cream silk scarf and her wavy hair hung over her shoulders, tousled and carefree.

'I'm Davla and this is my place,' she said, gesturing towards the café. 'You want to come in? Get out of this heat?'

She didn't wait for a reply, she simply went into the café, and expected me to follow her, which of course, I did.

***

'Why did you follow her?' Pieter asked me suddenly, interrupting me. 'Was it instinct or just curiosity?'

'I'm not sure,' I said. 'I think it was a bit of both. And I know this sounds strange but this beautiful butterfly followed her in. I've always had a thing for butterflies, so I saw that as a welcoming sign, to, you know, go in.'

Pieter laughed and told me I was too superstitious. I knew then that he could never completely understand the experience that I'd gone through. My grandmother had just died and that single event had thrown my whole life into turmoil. My job for a major university had been the most important thing in my life up until then. Suddenly writing about the successes of the students, attending lectures after work and liaising with the student union became tedious and hard work.

I had never told him that my mother called.

'I was still asleep. She called early in the morning and said that my grandmother had just passed away.'

I turned to look at Pieter; he was listening to me intently.

I remember getting the call very early. It must have been around four in the morning. Her voice sounded small on the phone.

'Get a cab, come home' she'd said. Her voice was cracking. She handed the phone to my father. He said: 'It's your nan. She's dead, Nina.' He sounded so tired, as if he were ready to collapse himself. As if the burden of saying those words was beginning to sink in.

'Pieter, I knew he was trying to stay strong for my mother's sake. I promised him I'd get a cab and be over in a short while, but I remember that I took my time, as strong emotions churned inside me. For almost an hour, I replayed my mothers' voice repeating those words, I just couldn't move. I stared at the ceiling, feeling nauseous; my heart pounding. Images of nan raced through my head.'

***

Apparently, she'd had a relapse of the ovarian cancer that the doctors had found years ago. At that time, they had caught it early and she had a few chemotherapy treatments. The whole family had arrived in Delhi to help her. She had surprised everyone by rapidly improving and remarkably soon, she was well again. A year later, she had visited

London and stayed at my mother's house. I'd visited her almost every day for a month and it had been a joy to see her. The cancer coming back so unexpectedly was a cruel shock.

***

'The beginning of my world was starting to collapse,' I told Pieter. 'She was my pillar of strength and I hadn't known it until then.'

'Why didn't you tell me any of this at the time?' Pieter asked.

'It was too difficult and I was trying to make sense of it all myself. We still didn't know each other too well either,' I added.

Pieter nodded slowly, he looked perplexed. 'What happened next?' he asked.

'Well, I took time off work and flew to Delhi. From there we travelled to my uncle's house in Varanasi. The idea of my grandmother's ashes being thrown into the river Ganges, like confetti in the wind, filled me with infinite sadness. I recalled when we'd laughed together standing on the roof of her house in Delhi. Now all perspective of time faded away. It occurred to me how short life really was and for a moment, the whole idea of existence seemed absurd. I had asked myself the same question I had throughout different periods in my life, what was the point of it all?'

Pieter moved his chair closer to mine as I remembered and took my hand in his. His warmth seeped through me and I smiled.

'You didn't tell me she was scattered in the Ganges! I always thought she was buried in Delhi, I think cremation is so, I don't know – final...' he said.

'It doesn't matter whether a loved one is buried or cremated, that person has gone,' I said.

Pieter nodded and asked me to continue.

'When we arrived back in London, my parents insisted that I move back in with them, but I refused. Instead I spent time with my colleagues in different bars or dated men I really did not care about.'

'Did you really?' Pieter said, raising his eyebrows.

'Yes,' I answered. 'It was all a distraction. The drinking stopped me thinking about nan. Often when I returned to my flat, the loneliness would start to seep in, dulled by the red wine that I'd consumed. Eventually however, I tired of it all.'

'You mean your life became predictable,' Pieter said. 'What happened after you met Davla then?'

***

Once I'd followed Davla inside the café, I noticed a small sign near the door, stuck on the glass indicating that there was a room available to rent in a local shared flat. It was written on a luminous pink post-it note and there was a mobile number at the bottom. I'd been thinking about moving out of my flat in West London and this seemed like the perfect opportunity. Next to the ad was a small poster with a picture of a tarot card, the Empress, I think. It said: *Tarot readings available, £10 for 20 minutes, £25 for an hour.*

I looked around inside the café, taking everything in with a glance. The place was small, cosy and inviting, yet hardly trendy. It was furnished indifferently, as if someone had decided to throw together any furniture they could find. There was a sense of unhurriedness about it, as if time stood still there. The café seemed cut off from the street outside, a womblike world that felt safe.

***

'It sounds very welcoming,' Pieter said, interrupting me. I wasn't sure if he was being serious.

'Yes, it was. And it felt familiar somehow, as if I'd walked into a place I already knew. There was a feeling of déjà vu about it, as if I'd just met an old friend whom I hadn't seen for years, but who was exactly the same when we reunited.'

'It sounds like a magical place,' Pieter said.

'Exactly, and I also saw the butterfly that had flown in perched on the mirror, so that it reflected like two butterflies. It was beautiful and for some reason I couldn't stop thinking of nan and I felt emotional. I felt as if she'd guided me from wherever she was into that place and that thought never left my mind.'

'So you felt compelled to stay there?' Pieter asked.

'Yes, it would have been wrong to leave when she felt so, well, close,' I said.

***

The café had six tables, two were square, one was oval and three were round and different in size. Around the tables were red, black and white stools, which I liked. Unlit candles were on the centre of each table. As it was still bright, the only light on was behind the small glass counter. Sandwich fillings lay behind it in neat containers. I could see mayonnaise and mozzarella. Fresh French bread stood in a basket at the side of the counter.

The back of the café had mirrors all the way across the side. Perhaps in an attempt to make it look bigger.

For a moment, I caught my reflection and I was surprised at how tired I looked. It seemed the past few months had taken their toll.

The café was quiet apart from the sound of the coffee machine. Davla straightened her hair in the mirror behind me and applied a fresh coat of red lipstick.

'Anyway, what can I get for you? I've just made a fresh pot of Brazilian coffee.'

'Coke is fine, thanks,' I told her.

'This weather reminds me of back home and then I miss my friends again in Sao Paulo.'

As she turned to get my coke, I tried to work out how old she was. She must have been in her early thirties.

She poured my coke over a glass half filled with ice and a slice of lemon, it bubbled up to the top. I sipped my drink and looked out of the window.

***

'One visit to nan was when I was twelve years-old,' I told Pieter. 'On this particular night, I was sleeping on one end of a large room on an uncomfortable bed and nan was sleeping on the opposite side on a small bed that was made especially for her. I woke up at dawn to see her lighting some incense after she'd opened the window. She didn't know that I was awake. The smell of incense scented the air.'

'You mean that was her daily ritual, first thing?' Pieter asked.

'Yes, it was and afterwards, she would read the Bhagavad Gita, the Bible or the Koran, all of which lay on a shelf near the window. She liked to alternate the religious books depending on what took her fancy. She would pick up the incense sticks and swirl them in the air as if they could magically cleanse it. She never told me that she practised this ritual. The last time I visited her a year ago, I told her that I'd seen her get up several times to light the incense and pray.'

'I always knew you were awake,' she'd laughed softly. 'But it wasn't you I was thinking about at that hour. I had to welcome the day and say thanks to God that I was around to see it.'

***

Davla was greeting another customer who had just come in. He was a man about sixty years old. The first thing I noticed about him was that he wore a purple bow tie. They greeted each other warmly, and she gave him a kiss on the cheek. He saw me looking, so I smiled. His eccentric looks and clothes intrigued me. He wore a cream coloured shirt, and a smart cream blazer.

He bought a cup of tea and then came up to me and asked if he could sit with me. I hesitated and he peered at me from behind his steel rimmed glasses.

'Of course, that's fine,' I said.

He smiled and sat down beside me.

'How do you know Davla?' he asked me, after a short pause.

I explained that I'd only just stopped by today.

In my mind, I had already concluded that he was somewhat eccentric. But I liked eccentric people, and he had an openness to him that was refreshing. He adjusted himself on the stool and then looked at me expectantly.

I stuck out my hand and he shook it. 'I'm Nina,' I said.

'James,' he said.

Davla was standing behind James, with her arms folded, listening to our conversation.

'James is a regular here,' Davla said. 'We've discussed so many issues together that I'm surprised we haven't solved the world's problems! We certainly should have done, by now.'

'That's true, we've talked about all manner of things.' James chuckled. 'By the way, has anyone asked about my spare room?'

'No one yet,' Davla said, shaking her head. 'Did anyone call you about it?'

'Well, I've had a couple of unknown numbers on my phone,' James said. 'Which wasn't helpful to me.'

'Is that the vacant room advertised in the window?' I asked.

'Yes, it's close to here,' James said. 'Were you interested in looking at it?'

'I might well be,' I said.

James smiled. 'Let's discuss it later.'

'Good thing you stepped in here today then,' Davla said.

Her eyes glanced outside, where she watched the people walk by. Two men stopped and waved at her. She excused herself and rushed outside to greet them.

'As Davla was saying, we love to debate in this place,' James said. 'Last week we discussed the philosopher Kierkegaard – Davla didn't like him, too religious for her! She's into Nietzsche and she thought God must be dead too otherwise she couldn't understand why there is so much suffering in the world. That old chestnut again! You don't know how many times I hear people say that.'

'So, you believe in God?'

'I do indeed, young lady!'

'Are you religious then?'

'You can call it that, I suppose. I became a spiritual person four years ago, when my wife died. Before that I was too dogmatic and maybe I still am sometimes.' He shrugged and smiled.

'What does God mean to you exactly?' I asked, curiously. For some reason, I felt I could trust this man. It seemed to me that he held deep values that many did not care about any more.

'I believe that God is an energy that is inside us and also outside us, if you see what I'm getting at. God is inside a person because he gives that person strength through their faith – whatever the faith is. That person will recognise that the space in his heart is for God. Yet God is also outside of you because you have to invite him in. Does this make sense?'

His voice trailed off. I must have looked sad because he suddenly patted my arm gently.

'James, you're going to hate me but I have to ask you, why *does* a loving God let people suffer?'

I thought of my nan, of her passing and the familiar feeling of loss tugged at me again. I remembered her ashes disappearing forever into the Ganges like tricks of light played on the water.

'That's a hard one, but my understanding is that it is us who create that suffering. We can turn against each other and against ourselves.

'God's love is beyond our understanding but it does manifest itself in glimpses in our world. That love can be felt through other people who may not be your family – it's all about learning who we are and what our journey in life is. I think this also helps us understand and change ourselves to be more in line with our spiritual side. I believe that God has also protected me throughout my life. I don't want to get too personal right now, but I've had people influenced by dark forces trying to put spells on me.'

'Really?' I wasn't sure whether he was joking or not.

'God has protected me from black magic and evil people. Magic isn't just about David Copperfield you know, or pulling rabbits out of hats!' He sipped his tea.

'Aren't you going a little too far now?' I asked.

'Nina, all I'm going to say is that I believe there is a reason for everything and that if I wasn't as strong as I am now, that black magic could have harmed me. God is love and if we all *understood* that, this world would be a different place, most likely a much better one. I would say I'm a Christian.'

He straightened his bow-tie, and then chuckled. He seemed to be enjoying himself. I wondered if he often chatted to strangers at random.

'Do you believe in anything?' he asked.

I started to say no, but told him maybe.

'I've been thinking about God a lot more now than I used to.'

'Well, that's a good start,' he said, sipping his tea.

I glanced outside. Davla was laughing with the mystery men and one of them put his arm around her. I felt a pang of loneliness and jealousy echo through me at how free she seemed. I was too troubled by the death of my nan to flirt with anyone at that time, it hardly mattered. Lately, I hadn't been interested in dating or relationships. Now, watching Davla, it became apparent that another part of my life was missing. I wondered if I would ever experience love of the kind that I was seeking, instead of empty flings.

***

'I didn't know you'd had a fling with that David Lane guy!' Pieter said, bringing up an old colleague of mine. I assured him that we had only kissed one night after a work do, but he wanted to know more.

'Is there anything else that I need to know?' he asked, half mockingly.

'There really isn't,' I said and he laughed.

James' voice cut through my thoughts again and I returned to my story.

***

'Ever since I first came in here, Davla has always had a lot of male attention,' James told me.

'She's a beautiful woman,' I said.

I was fascinated by his thoughts, which seemed to be as interesting as his dress sense.

James noticed me looking at him and he took his glasses off so that I could see his face more clearly. It was kind and yet haughty. His pale blue eyes shone enigmatically. There was a mystery to his personality, as if he had innate knowledge of a world I had never encountered but was on the brink of discovering. It was like a map to a place where I'd never been.

His hair was thinning and grey on top, and it was slicked down neatly, as if he'd made a real effort. I noticed that his ears stuck out, but he was trying to disguise them by pulling his hair over them, as if they embarrassed him.

'This place is like a second home to me,' he said. 'I can relax here and talk to the others or chat up Davla, when she's in a good mood! You name me another café where I can do that!'

He raised his eyebrows slightly and laughed.

He glanced at Davla again. As he watched her, his manner changed briefly. It was as if he remembered something, he looked thoughtful for a second.

'What do you do, James?' I asked him. 'If you don't mind me speculating, I think you're a teacher.'

The look that came over his face made me laugh out loud. He looked genuinely bewildered.

'How on earth did you know that?'

'It's just a wild guess!'

'Well, it's a bloody good one, young lady! I was a teacher, actually,' he said. 'For thirteen years. It was good, but it wasn't what I wanted forever.'

I looked at Davla again outside. She was now deep in conversation with both men and was gesturing like mad. Suddenly she said something and everyone laughed. After kissing them goodbye, she came back in, looking much brighter than before.

She turned to serve a customer, but the man only wanted directions to Piccadilly Circus.

'The amount of times people come in here asking the way,' she sighed. 'I may as well start charging for my services.'

'That will be a great way to bring extra money into the café!' James laughed out loud.

Davla pulled a face of mock sarcasm at him, and started singing softly, as she turned back to the counter. She began straightening out the KitKats in their cardboard boxes. The funny thing was they were already in order. The tension became palpable in the café. A moment ago, talking to the two young men, she had been lively. Now the boredom was settling in again and a feeling of frustration seemed to settle over the place.

James had also noticed the shift in Davla's mood. She turned back around to the corner where the CD player sat, and walked out of my sight.

I wouldn't have noticed the couple of bookshelves behind me, if James hadn't pointed them out. He mentioned that he had read quite a few of the books there. An astrology book caught my attention and a copy of the Bhagavad Gita stood out, a version for Westerners. It was my nan's favourite spiritual book. To her, it was the epic song of God, and she had sometimes made references to Krishna as the speaker of the Bhagavad Gita.

There were also some art books and collected works by Carl Jung. At the end of the last shelf, a high pile of tarot cards looked as if they would topple over and fall delicately to the ground, in a colourful heap of knights, chariots, towers and lovers.

Davla came back after turning on the radio. The music was loud and chirpy; an artificial sounding dance beat that masked the world inside her.

She started cleaning one of the tables behind us, polishing the dark blue surface.

'Those books on the shelf look interesting,' I said to her. 'And those tarot cards, are you really into astrology?'

'Yes,' she answered, suddenly brightening. 'I do tarot readings too. You can always get a quick one.'

She took the cards from the shelf and asked me to shuffle them for a few minutes. She presented them to me upside down so I couldn't see them. I shuffled them and handed her the pack.

'Right, let's see what's happening with you, I can see that in the first three cards.'

She flipped them over.

'Okay, we start with the Queen of Cups, that's you. Cups is emotions, I'd say something is making you emotional at the moment. The six of cups, interesting, more cups! That means you're on a journey of some kind and you'll need a lot of energy for this. And you see there's a baby in this card too? That means you're new to all of this, you haven't been on this road before.'

She turned the last card.

'The high priestess, that's a great card.' She sounded surprised and looked over at me quickly, smiling.

'That's actually a very spiritual card, it's someone who attains wisdom and understanding eventually.'

'Perhaps you're secretly doing a reading about me,' James interrupted, laughing. 'I'd like to think I've attained some kind of wisdom in my old age!'

'James, this isn't about you,' Davla said and James stopped laughing.

'Here take a look.' Davla handed me the card.

It fit neatly into the palm of my hand. In the picture, a woman was standing in a blue cloak which fell softly over a medieval red robe and a golden belt hugged her waist. In her hands she carried a big red book bound in gold cover, her face was tilted towards the book as if it contained a great secret. She was wearing a simple yellow cloth around her head. Behind her, two trees towered above on either side.

I was intrigued by the beauty of the cards and by what they appeared to be saying.

'I don't personally believe in those readings,' James said. 'They are in opposition to God.'

'James, one day you'll have to give me a good explanation as to why the cards contradict God,' Davla said. 'I mean, it's possible to read tarot and still believe in God, are you saying that I don't?'

'I'm saying that those cards are linked to the occult,' James said.

'James, I thought you said you believed in black magic earlier,' I said. 'Isn't that also the occult?'

James looked at me surprised that I had spoken up. Davla smiled and continued cleaning the tables.

'I didn't mean it was a good thing,' he said, his face flushed. 'What people don't know is always scary,' Davla said.

'It's each to their own, my dear,' James said.

He turned to me and asked me if I still wanted to find out about the vacant room in his flat. I said I would and he asked if I was free now.

I said yes and he hastily added that the room was only available for a few months over the summer.

***

I turned to Pieter; he was listening to me attentively.

'You were going to move in with a complete stranger?' Pieter asked, looking at me quizzically. He looked at the menu and ordered a pizza. 'If this guy is as religious as he sounds, I would have advised you strongly against it.'

I laughed and said that James was harmless.

'Pieter, you don't know how I felt then; I was different to how I am now. I'm complete with you, but back then, I was drifting. Nan had just died. My life seemed pointless. The café and James were there at the right time, they both helped me to grow up.'

'Why did you need the café?' Pieter asked and the abruptness of his voice surprised me. I assumed he was just hungry. 'What was so great about the place?'

'I was lonely. All those friends I thought I had, it was all an illusion – they were superficial,' I said and I felt a resonance within me when I told him. 'For too long, I'd been doing what I thought I was *supposed* to be doing, you know, hanging out and being sociable and pretending that everything was fine. It was a house of cards that could collapse at any time and that's what happened. When nan died, it made me realise that none of it was important and life was too bloody short.'

***

James was watching me as I slipped off my stool. His hands, like his face, were like a record of who he was. They told a tale of hardship, and tireless strain and wear and tear. Nan claimed that she could read the life of someone by palm reading; she had looked at mine once, when I was a child. A long life and lots of luck, she had said. But grandmothers always say those kinds of things, don't they? They try to cushion you and make you feel safe. Nan had a funny and quiet way of getting her messages across to me. I didn't realise it then, being only a youngster, but now I knew the seeds she'd planted had grown.

She told me to observe people from afar. It was enough to read them, like open books. It was all about energy, she said, *everything* was energy. Nan understood people, she could look beyond what they said and how they acted; she could see them for who they really were.

A man's world is in his hands, she had said once. Looking now at James' hands, I believed her. There was something extraordinary embedded into those knuckles. One cut seemed painful and deep. The fingers were slightly thick; a ring on the index finger appeared to be a little tight. The light hairs on the back of the hands were dark. Strength emanated from the fingers, a quiet strength that had helped him in troubled times.

James began to tap the fingers of his left hand impatiently on the table. He cleared his throat, and I looked up. He pulled his hands towards him, and crossed them over his chest, hiding them. He must have seen me staring.

'I thought we were going to see my room, *are we?*' he asked, his tone sharp.

He looked at me curiously. He was evaluating what it would be like to live with me, a stranger.

A young woman walked into the café and asked Davla if she could give her a reading. She became busy and we stepped outside.

***

'Great, a Brazilian who reads tarot and runs a café,' Pieter interrupted me, suddenly. 'What kind of a circus café was this place, anyway?'

'It was not a circus!' I said, indignantly. 'It was the place where I really understood how shallow my bloody life had become. I knew if I didn't change it, I would never be happy.'

Pieter looked at me with his caring look that always had the effect of calming me. Since the death of his mother recently, we understood each other even more. I knew he wasn't going to leave me, like some of the other men I had encountered. He was reliable and stable. As I looked into his blue eyes, I realised that for the first time in my life, I was in love.

'When I first met you, Pieter, I'd felt an immediate connection with you and I knew that you were the right man for me. I had never experienced that before.'

Pieter smiled. 'That's nice, darling. Well, I'm sorry old James isn't there today. I'd have liked to have met him.' He looked over at the dark windows of the café opposite. 'Although, I have to admit the café looks like its time is really over now.'

***

As James and I left, we saw Davla sitting at a table, with a host of tarot cards strewn over the surface. The woman was sitting close to her, her eyes fixed on the cards.

'I only caught the end of your reading,' James said, turning to me. 'Did she say anything else interesting the rest of the time?'

'She told me I was on a journey.'

'Well, we're all on a journey, my dear.' James laughed. 'Mine is mostly on the RV1 bus from Covent Garden to South Bank!'

James and I walked back to his flat. Along the way, he was talkative at first but eventually he became so preoccupied that he almost forgot I was there.

He began staring ahead of him, his face impassive and sad, like an old statue that no one noticed any more. I joked about him getting too serious and he playfully gave me a punch on my arm and told me that we had almost arrived at his front door.

CHAPTER THREE

James' small flat off Tavistock Street was only a two minute walk from Covent Garden. The vacant room was large and immaculately kept.

It was painted lilac and I found the colour immediately calming. A rich purple satin sheet decorated with large dark green embroidered flowers lay over a light duvet on the bed. The dark wooden floorboards had a large sheepskin rug in the centre and a black leather chair stood close by. I sat down and tilted it back, resting my feet on the front.

'This is fantastic, James.'

He smiled and pointed out that I could place my clothes in the large mahogany wardrobe opposite the bed.

'That was Angie, my wife's wardrobe,' James said. 'I had it specially made for her.'

'It's lovely,' I said and he smiled.

My side table had a beautiful lamp from Africa with a giraffe silhouette. A large print of Van Gogh's *sunflowers* in a gold chunky frame hung over the bed. The room felt warm and the smell of incense rose in the air, freshly, as if he'd lit it a moment ago.

***

'That smell reminded me of the incense my nan used to burn in India,' I said to Pieter. 'And that's when I knew I had to have that room!'

***

'I hope you don't mind the jasmine incense?' James said as if he were reading my mind.

He was standing just inside the room watching me. The door creaked as it slowly closed behind. He opened the wooden blind and the sun streamed through the window, bathing the room with a rosy glow.

'Well, this is it,' he said. 'The rent is reasonable and I'd prefer short term to start with. Do you think it's suitable?'

'How soon can I move in?'

He seemed taken aback then laughed suddenly, offering to show me the rest of the flat and make me a cup of tea.

***

'That was a bit fast, wasn't it?' Pieter interrupted me. 'Did you really think it was the best thing to do, move in with this old guy? I'm surprised that you made such a decision, Nina. You normally weigh things up pretty well.'

'Absolutely, it was the right decision.' I realised I sounded defensive, so I took a deep breath and calmed down. 'I wouldn't have done it otherwise! There was something about this man that I needed to understand, indeed, it seemed I was destined to.'

Pieter asked me to continue my story.

***

I followed James into the small, dark kitchen and he made me a cup of tea. There was an immaculately clean cooker and small fridge. Next to the window, a wooden table was covered with clear plastic on top of a blue coloured cloth. There were two small wooden chairs on either side of the table, tucked away neatly underneath it.

Perched on the table were a box of cornflakes, a box full of tea bags and half a baguette. A mug had the words *world's greatest teacher*, written on a cartoon blackboard, with an animated smiling teacher with goofy teeth pointing to it.

'You can keep your food there,' James said, pointing at a shelf near the cooker. A strange loneliness lingered in the kitchen, the stench of someone who lived alone.

He had lived here now for four years since his wife died, and there was still an air of loneliness in the place. Even as we left the kitchen and walked into the living room, the very words, *living room*, became a source of irony. There was a sense of urgency there, as if everything in the room were trying to find an answer to a question long forgotten. It was as if all the objects had a story to tell and a thousand voices wanted to speak at once.

Every corner and every wall, even the ceiling itself, with its large white chandelier, seemed to be burdened. The bookshelves suggested that James was obsessed by books of all shapes and sizes. Several were stacked precariously on top of each other, ready to topple over.

To the right of the door was a cream leather sofa and on the left was a wooden desk with fountain pens and pale blue paper sprawled over the surface. A lamp was attached to the side and behind it was a small chair, just big enough for one person.

James motioned for me to sit on the sofa.

The wall behind him was like a shrine to his wife. Photographs of them both together overlapped each other. The clearest one on top showed them with their arms around each other in a place with blue skies. It looked like a beach but the image was grainy. There were souvenirs from their travels on the mantelpiece. A small plastic Eiffel Tower, foreign coins, a fridge magnet from Spain with a flamenco dancer. I walked over to get a closer look.

'She's in all of those photos, my Angie,' James said softly.

She had a distant smile in all the photographs, as if she'd been thinking about something else when the camera had flashed.

In one photo, perhaps ten years old, James and his wife stood close with their arms around each other. They were sitting on a beach with the sea in the background.

'That was in Dalaman in Turkey.'

'It looks like you were having a wonderful time.'

'That *was* definitely the best holiday. She was the love of my life, what can I say?' James laughed.

'Anyway, you haven't seen the bathroom yet. Not that there's much to see. Well, there are some lovely tiles from Morocco.'

He picked up a cardboard frame that was on the television. When he turned it around, I saw a photograph. A sea of smiling faces, all teenage boys in navy school uniform looked up at me. Standing in the midst of them was James.

'This class photo was taken about twelve years ago now!' he said, his voice bursting with pride. He wiped some dust off the edges of the frame, along the faded gold line that ran through the black.

'This is a great photo, James. I mean you really *were* a teacher.'

'Of course, I was!' he said. 'Did you think I was making it up?'

'No, it's just that, well, this picture just brings it home.'

He nodded, and his face softened. 'Once a teacher, always a teacher. Sometimes it's like I'm there again, back in that classroom, always with something to say.'

'Don't you miss it?' I asked.

'Now and then, I suppose I do.'

He looked sad and suggested that we go out for a walk.

'I often go to Speakers' Corner in Hyde Park on Sundays,' he said. 'Perhaps you'd like to join me?'

'I haven't been there for a while, but why not?' I said. He smiled at me and we got up and left together.

***

'So now you're going for walks with strange men?' Pieter asked. 'I hope this wasn't a habit of yours.' I could not tell if he was joking or genuinely offended.

The waitress came over and we ordered a bottle of red wine.

'I can assure you it wasn't,' I said. 'I felt comfortable with James. It was very similar to how I used to feel with nan.'

***

I remembered nan standing on the open roof of the house in Delhi the last time I had visited her. A gust of wind caught the white scarf she was wearing around her neck and blew it lightly so that it fluttered like a kite in the air. We were standing together looking at the city around us in the early morning, with our cup of chai, freshly made by Anita the housekeeper, and already the heat was rising. Nan told me she had started painting classes and one of my rich uncles, the manager of an international hotel chain, had organised for her to have English learning classes every week. My Hindi was rusty, so we spoke in a combination of both.

I saw the Jama Mosque in the distance, the finest and largest in India. For my nan, this was everyday scenery, for me it was pretty amazing and a million times better than opening my curtains in my former flat in Ealing and finding Mr Khan's small corner shop opposite the road, piled up outside with boxes of fruit and vegetables.

***

The rush of tourists in Oxford Street and the heat became too much for me and James after a while on our way to Hyde Park. I hadn't been here for a while and now I noticed all kinds of people present. Everyone from Londoners to day trippers, families from different backgrounds, trendsetters and old couples.

The constant stream of people was tiring, but there was no escape from the crowds. James suggested taking a bus, but they were all packed and traffic was moving too slowly. So we decided to walk. People blocked our path as they rushed towards us, always frantic. The walk from Oxford Circus to Marble Arch seemed to be taking far too long. The static pollution hanging in the air, made my throat dry. The cold water that I had bought only half an hour earlier was already getting tepid in my bag.

Speakers' Corner – the melting pot of debate, heated exchanges and ideas – was the highlight of the week for some of the speakers who visited. It was the one day when the world listened to them and they became the centre of attention, and today it was already in full swing.

Tourists snapped away with their cameras. Speakers stood on small ladders, crates or on the ground. They were all here, Muslims, Jews, Christians, members of the Socialist party, a Palestinian waving his country's flag, and an old man carrying a banner that said, *Jesus is coming back soon, look busy.*

The anticipation of the crowds was strong; I felt it as I walked amongst them. It was like a mini circus, the speakers performed their acts, the crowd clapped or booed. I recognised some of the speakers from my previous visits. I had enjoyed listening to some of the lively debates and had even participated in a few.

Once, a Christian man from Africa in a long white gown had asked me who my God was. He had assumed that I was a Hindu because of my jangling gold Indian bracelets, a gift from my nan.

'Aren't Hindus polytheists? Everything is a God to them! Probably even that tree you just passed by, tell me daughter are you a Hindu too?' the African man had asked me.

I'd stopped in my tracks, surprised at his address.

'Sorry, I think you're getting me confused with someone else, I'm not religious,' I had replied, feeling my face getting hot.

'Ah, but wait a minute...'

He had paused and started flipping the pages of the hard back Bible in his hands. He'd pointed at me in an ominous way.

'Daughter, you are here today to be reborn. Jesus died for your sins. I say you are here today, *to be reborn,* no one knows the hour or day that he will come back, so keep watch.'

His voice became louder and soon he was shouting and spit started flying out of the corner of his mouth. At that point I had hastily started walking away. A tourist couple took a photograph of him pointing at me again. The encounter had put me off coming for a while.

Now here I was again and it seemed that nothing much had changed. There was Leon, a funny Jewish guy, who usually had a huge crowd. I had spoken to him a few times and he mostly talked about sex, especially in the modern day marriage.

Leon usually stood on a small ladder, and gestured wildly at people in the crowd. If any policemen happened to approach and he was talking about sex at the time, he'd very quickly start to talk about religion, at the precise moment when they walked past. It was all part of the act, and the policemen were always left nonplussed at the peals of laughter from the crowd.

***

'Leon did ask me out a couple of times,' I told Pieter. 'But he just wasn't my type. He was short, balding and he came across as being desperate, somehow. And anyway, I can't fancy a man who makes jokes about biscuit crumbs falling on his private parts.'

Pieter laughed. 'I'm really relieved to hear that, Nina,' he said.

***

That day with James, there were even more speakers than usual.

I walked past tourists with cameras around their necks, past the old man waiting for Jesus.

James had started a conversation with a Chinese lady and she was asking him what branch of Christianity he belonged to.

'Hang on there, you still haven't explained to me your last statement. What is the point of your beliefs if you don't live in accordance with them?' James asked, impatiently.

'Are you judging me now?' the woman asked, her voice rising.

'Let's go,' James said to me. He had lost interest and was asking me if I wanted a drink or an ice-cream.

'An ice-cream would be great.'

We started to walk towards the stall.

'Some people here are nuts,' James said. 'Like that woman. I mean talk about giving a dog a bone to chew on.'

I laughed and he said that he would go to church later that evening.

He bought us mint ice-creams.

'I don't usually get involved with all the speakers,' I said. 'I think Leon's good because he doesn't talk about religion as much.'

There was now hardly any room to sit on the grass near Speakers' Corner. People were sitting on hired deck chairs, listening to a guy softly playing an acoustic guitar. He looked up as we walked past, and winked at me. James didn't notice and we sat down on the grass at a relatively quiet spot. He took an empty, neatly folded plastic bag from his pocket. He carefully unfolded it and then sat down on it. There were a few people playing football not far from us and we could hear them calling out names.

'Anyway, I'm convinced that woman has it all wrong,' James said, turning to face me.

'Who?'

'Oh, that little Chinese woman I was just speaking to.'

'Do you really find that heavy talk engaging *every* Sunday?'

'It's not heavy talk,' James said, suddenly perking up and staring at me, his eyes bright and alert as a sparrow's. 'It's *necessary*. You young people don't know anything nowadays.'

He said it with such force that I stared at him, surprised.

'No, I suppose we don't,' I said, finally. 'Anyway, I'm thirty. I'm not even that young anymore and now I'm open to ideas.'

His tone softened. 'I just don't know what young people find important these days, do you?'

'Well, I can't speak for every young person and of course, we're all different. Right now, I've had enough of partying and I'd like some life experience, something meaningful, you know?'

'Ah, hence our conversation about God, you must be getting old my dear.'

'More grown up, you mean?'

'You could say that young lady.'

He was watching a couple kissing a short distance away.

'I used to be like that once,' he said. 'I was terribly in love with Angela and then God took her away and I lost my best friend.'

'What happened?'

'She died four years ago, and do you know, it could just as well be last week. Time can heal some things but the pain doesn't go. Will you look at that?' he said suddenly, pointing at a brown butterfly that was perfectly still on the grass close to him.

'That's the second one I've seen this summer. The other one was in the café,' I said.

'Really, maybe we've got a butterfly boom this year and there's more out there.' He paused. 'Nina, have you ever had anyone close to you pass away?'

'Yes,' I answered. 'My nan's house had always been a home away from home for me. It was like that after her funeral, I remember climbing the stairs to the second floor, to the small room where she'd kept her private letters and photographs. I almost fancied she walked up with me and her hand was on mine as the great rusty lock on the door reluctantly slid open, so that I could enter.

'Once inside, I switched the light on and the dim bulb cast a shadow on the wall opposite me. I breathed in the musty air as the outline of several shelves in front of me became apparent. They were piled up with old suitcases and boxes. I looked up, half expecting to see the butterfly again, the special one I had seen when I was ten years old. In my memories, it was clear still and it was in that room with nan.'

***

'Which butterfly was that?' Pieter asked me, topping up my glass with more wine.

'Funny, that's what James asked me.'

'And what did you tell him?'

'I told him that I've adored butterflies since I was a young girl. Just the way they transformed from a caterpillar into butterflies, there's something really magical about that. It's like a dance, if you like.'

'Was the one in the room with your grandmother dancing?' Pieter asked, grinning. His comment irritated me, but I said nothing. The wine was making me relaxed. 'That's a funny thing to say, as if it was putting on a personal performance just for you.'

'Yes, it felt like that when I was ten,' I said and Pieter urged me to continue.

***

James was more pensive than earlier. It seemed there was a shadow over his personality, like an eclipse of the sun.

'You know, I was with Angela for fifteen years. I met her at Victoria Station, of all places. It happens, in the space of a few minutes life can suddenly change.

'I saw this woman and I knew that I had to ask her for a cup of coffee, so that's what I did. I simply stopped her in the street and asked her to join me. She laughed and asked me why she should have a drink with me, a complete stranger. Anyway, I convinced her that she should and three hours later we were still in the café, talking our hearts out.'

'That sounds incredible,' I said. 'Why did you pick her?'

'I don't know. Call it fate if you like.'

We sat there quietly for a moment with the gentle breeze blowing in between the trees.

'What's it like living in the heart of London?' I asked.

'It's convenient and it's nice to have London as your backyard. I'm sorry about your grandmother. Is that why you fancy a move from your flat in Ealing?' he asked.

'Yes, I seem to be outgrowing a lot of things lately.'

'Oh,' he said, looking at me curiously, before changing the subject. 'Do you like music?'

I said yes and he told me that he liked romantic music.

***

'Well, that's a good chat up line.' Pieter interrupted my story; the wine was making him a little boisterous. 'Are you sure he didn't have a thing for you?'

'Yes, I'm certain. Are you jealous of an old man I met five years ago? Look, he was into his jazz, he mentioned the Soho Jazz festival and that he was keen to go. James was so hung up about his wife that I don't think anyone else mattered.'

Pieter nodded and backed off, he looked at the darkened windows of the café again.

'It's really a shame that he isn't around now,' he said again.

***

James told me he was a good singer.

'Name me a song, any one you like and I'll sing it for you,' he joked.

'Just sing one of your favourites.'

I was sure he was joking, but he started to sing *Strangers in the night*. His voice was light yet strong and perfectly in tune. At one point, he held his arms out in one long exaggerated sweep. His gestures made me laugh and he began laughing himself.

'What do you think about that, it's not bad is it?'

'It's not actually,' I said and I meant it.

His hand caressed the grass gently and the sensuality of his movements, the caring way in which he smoothed a leaf out from under his palm, it was like he was touching the curve of a lover's back.

'I used to sing to Angela all the time,' he said. 'She used to laugh at my singing when I'd had one too many.'

We sat there for quite a while, the shade of the tree sheltering us. I was aware of people coming and going, families and lovers, players and runners, people on roller blades in the distance. Hyde Park belonged to everyone, but today it seemed that we had a small part of it for ourselves.

James told me how he had given up his teaching to look after Angela when she became ill with breast cancer. After her death, he worked as a volunteer in a charity shop for a while.

Later, when I glanced at my watch, I realised with a start that we'd been sitting in Hyde Park for almost two hours.

I laughed and he asked me when I thought I could move into the spare room.

'How about a couple of days, would that be possible?'

James told me he would prepare a contract for the next evening and I agreed to sign it with a payment for the first month's rent.

***

'It was that fast,' I told Pieter. 'Luckily, I didn't have much furniture and what I did was put into safe storage. My friend wasn't pleased about me moving, but he could hardly stop me. Within three days, I arrived in my room in James' flat.'

'That was a very quick move,' Pieter said. 'Clearly, I had no idea about your life then. You seemed to be more reckless at that time.'

'More spontaneous, yes,' I corrected him. 'I guess married life makes things more routine,' I joked but he didn't laugh, so I continued with my story.

***

In my room in James' flat in central London, as I looked at my alien surroundings, at my belongings in labelled boxes, a wave of familiarity rushed over me.

I remembered being back in Delhi in that small room, amidst boxes around me then, as they were now. When I was ten, nan had taken me there and shown me her wedding dress. It was a lovely dark orange, with fine silver flowers embroidered along the sides.

The stillness of my new residence in Covent Garden reminded me of her room again after her death. Suddenly I missed nan's presence so deeply that something cut free inside.

I, who had been so stoic in Varanasi, so strong for my mother and myself, sat down on the bed in my new home and started to cry.

CHAPTER FOUR

James was an early riser and was usually out of the flat by the time I was up, which was just after eight thirty. He was mostly attending various academic talks at Westminster University or playing badminton with friends.

Following my move into his flat, I began to go to the café regularly, sometimes every day. I'd usually have a coffee and chat with Davla if she was free.

'Are you looking for work already? I thought you were taking the summer off?' she asked one day when she noticed me calling media agencies.

She cleaned the table next to me.

'I am but I don't want to get too slack.'

'Yes, good idea! Keep on top of it, darling.'

Davla was wearing a tight fitted denim shirt, tied in a huge knot at the front, which revealed her flat belly.

The radio was playing at a low volume. The door was open, and there was a constant stream of customers arriving.

'Darling, please can you give these two cokes to those love birds outside,' Davla said, winking at me.

When I came back an older couple were sitting at my table. The woman took out a small paper fan and fanned her face. She was sweating profusely.

'This weather is going to kill me,' she declared to the man sitting with her.

He didn't reply, he smiled at me instead as he drank his coffee.

He seemed too big for the café and his tall frame appeared cramped in the small place. Even as he sat on the stool with his long legs crossed in front of him, his brown leather roman sandals looked odd as his feet were very long. He must have been in his late forties.

I smiled back at him and the woman turned to look at me properly. She was in her fifties, although her face still looked quite young. Her skin was plump with a few freckles scattered across her upturned nose. Her grey hair was tied up firmly in a bun, but it was her eyes that really struck me. They were the colour of hazelnuts and looked vulnerable as if she had received bad news and was trying to digest it.

When she turned to look out of the window, her profile looked familiar. For a split second, my nan's face lingered before my eyes. But when I looked again, she looked nothing like nan.

***

'Did she look like her or not?' Pieter asked impatiently, interrupting me.

'I don't know if I was imagining it, but the resemblance was uncanny,' I answered.

'And then it changed, just like that?'

'Yes. It was almost like the café was playing tricks on me.'

'Well, someone was playing tricks on you.'

'I told you the café was a mysterious place, it was conjuring nan up in some way,' I said.

'Like a great magician at work? Nina, perhaps you were just missing her honey, in those early days after her death,' Pieter said.

'Pieter, that's not it. She was there, at least her spirit, energy, whatever you want to call it.'

Pieter nodded. 'Ok, that's a possibility, although I'm not sure I get that.'

I felt shaky for a moment, the tug of war conversation with Pieter was making me doubt myself, something I never did.

***

I closed my eyes and nan appeared in my mind. She took her hand in mine and it felt warm, we were standing back on the roof of her house and the sun was hot now. The sound of the street filled the air, the horns of the rickshaw drivers and the engines, disturbing the serenity of the moment. There was shouting in the streets below and the heat tickled my throat.

'One day I hope you'll remember us standing here,' Nan had said, laughing. 'And you'll be thinking of me. Nina, you're a very special young woman, you just don't know it yet.'

'Nan, you say that to everyone.'

'No, no dear, you don't understand. What you see here before you isn't the same as your life in London, is it now? I believe that you innately know what I already am familiar with about life and God.'

'What's that nan?' I laughed.

She laughed too and squeezed my hand. 'We all think we have a lot of time, child, but do we, really?'

When I looked at her she was sad, and looking back, I wonder if she had a premonition about her death that day, in the couple of years to follow.

'I love you Nan,' I said quickly.

'Me too my dear, just remember what I said. I mean that you are spiritual and you'll one day want to see your life in London beyond its pleasures.'

'That's natural, I suppose, it's called growing older.'

'It's called growing up,' she said.

The sun became too fierce after a while and we went inside.

***

'Do you work here?' the older woman in the café suddenly asked me rudely and my memories of nan vanished in an instant. 'I didn't know that Davla had hired more people.'

'I'm a newcomer, if you want to call it that, but I don't work here.'

'We come here all the time,' the man said, interrupting us. 'My name's Tony.' He stuck out a rather big hand, and I shook it. My hand seemed squashed by his large fingers.

'This place is like the hotel California, once you come in, you can never leave,' he said.

The woman looked at him and a flash of annoyance crossed her face.

'I'm Sarah, and you are?'

'Nina.'

'Well, Nina, what Tony *actually* means, is that we come to this café a lot because we go out around town and this is a convenient place to refuel.'

Tony had a sour expression on his face as he took a bite of his sandwich. His large hand held the baguette delicately and I wasn't sure if his fingers were shaking gently.

'We've just come from watching two delightful flamenco guitarists at the Royal Festival Hall,' Sarah said.

'Oh, they were awesome,' Tony agreed.

Together, Sarah and Tony seemed an odd couple and I wondered what they had in common.

***

'So now there are more strange people in this café.' Pieter blurted out, laughing. 'Where did James disappear to by the way?'

'He was out. He didn't always tell me where he was going. I was his lodger not his girlfriend.'

'You don't know how pleased I am to hear that,' Pieter said. 'Anyway, carry on Nina. I want to hear more.'

'Are you making fun of me?' I asked.

'No, I'm just interested in learning more about these people.' He nodded at the dim café across the road.

I continued after a huge gulp of wine.

***

'I see you've met the terrible twins.' Davla came over and smiled at me.

'I prefer the dynamic duo, which is what James called us the other day,' Sarah said

'So, you know James?' I asked Sarah.

'Of course, he's a regular.'

'I've just rented his spare room.'

'Oh, *you're* the new tenant he's been raving about.'

'Has he?'

'He thinks you're great. He's needed someone in there for a long time, been so lonely, poor chap.'

'It's nothing like that, I mean, I'm just his tenant.'

'Oh, I know that, what did you think I meant?'

'I'm not sure.' I could feel myself starting to blush. 'Does your husband know him as well?'

'You mean, Tony? He isn't my other half. Oh goodness, you are funny.' She started to laugh so hard that she had to put her fan down.

'We're *definitely* not married,' Tony chipped in. He seemed amused at Sarah's reaction.

'I've been there, done that and got the t-shirt. I had two kids, got divorced and I'm now ready to explore the rest of my life. Who needs marriage?' Sarah said.

'I don't believe in marriage either, a ring on my finger doesn't make me behave any differently,' Davla chipped in.

'Don't get me wrong, I do believe in marriage, I just married the wrong man. And now that I'm free again, I'm happy living out the rest of my days like this,' Sarah said.

She stood up and stepped over Tony's outstretched legs, which he refused to move. She walked around my stool, giving him a funny look as she did so.

'I'm going out to get some fresh air,' she said.

I haven't done anything to her, and still she keeps getting pissed off.

'Who does?' I asked Tony.

'Sorry?' he said.

'Did you just say something?'

Tony shifted on his stool with a searching look on his face.

'No,' he laughed.

'I could have sworn you just... well, it's none of my business, really.'

Tony looked really confused now.

'You must have misheard me as I haven't said anything at all in the last few minutes.'

***

'Let me get this straight, you're now hearing voices in the café?' Pieter asked me, interrupting again. 'Did they put something in your coffee, darling?'

'Actually, I was getting worried. I thought maybe I hadn't slept enough or I was imagining it. It was freaky, I have to say.'

'I'd see a doctor if I was hearing voices,' Pieter laughed.

I gave him a playful punch.

'Well, I've explained that there was something about the café, an energy that was different from any I've ever encountered. It felt extraordinarily alive in there, as if I was in a mini universe, exploring unknown territory. The understanding of a new world was opening up to me, one that I'd never experienced before. I'm telling you I heard Tony's voice speak to me as clearly as I'm seeing you now.'

'Why do you think that happened to you? I mean I can walk into Starbucks now and I'm sure that I wouldn't have such an awesome experience,' Pieter said.

'I can only refer to what nan told me. She thought I was gifted like her, that one day I would look beyond the here and now and search for a deeper understanding. It's like seeing another world beyond this one. It's not something I've been interested in so far and it's not rocket science, but now that she's gone, it's got me thinking about the meaning of life. If we were brutally honest with ourselves, everyone has asked if there is a God and why they are on the planet, haven't they? It's just that the conclusions we all come to are different, of course.'

'So you're tapping into a part of yourself that your nan said was always there?' Pieter leaned closer towards me, as if by doing that, he could see that part somehow. 'Did I miss something about you?'

'It's always been there. Maybe you never saw it, Pieter. I feel like I'm waking up from a long slumber I've been in for years.'

'Shit, so is there any hope for me?' Pieter said.

'This isn't exclusive to me. We can all access that part of ourselves if we choose to. Too many people don't though, so it remains untouched.'

Pieter gave me an uncertain look, as if he were trying to fathom my story and who I was.

'I love it when you look at me like that, it's so damn sexy.' I decided to be light hearted about it. 'It means you're taking me seriously,' I said.

He laughed. 'No, it means I'm *thinking* about what you're saying.'

'Well, keep thinking and I'll continue in the meantime.'

***

The café grew darker, as the sun momentarily went behind a cloud. With that, the atmosphere of the place appeared to change. People left and I moved over to another table and started to read a magazine. I didn't want to speak to Tony anymore. I was worried that I was hearing voices, that nan's death had affected me more than I realised. I sat there quietly, telling myself in my mind that everything was fine and I was well.

Davla cleaned the dirty tables and asked me if I wanted anything else to drink. I was so absorbed in my thoughts that I didn't hear her the first time.

'Nina, are you with us today?' she joked.

I giggled and just as I ordered another drink, Sarah rushed back in towards Tony.

'Did you see that man outside?' she asked him, breathlessly. Tony shook his head.

'You just missed him.' She sounded disappointed. 'He's an up and coming film director, and he's invited me to the opening of his film next week.'

Tony didn't say anything, but his face looked envious.

'We met at the London film festival last year,' Sarah went on.

She came back to the table, where her bag was still lying.

'Oh, you've moved, did we annoy you that much?' she said to me.

I started to say no and Davla bought my order over, and relieved, I returned to reading my magazine.

A hush descended on the café, at the same time as the sun broke through the clouds and the place became lighter again. It seemed as if everyone in the café had stopped talking at once, it became quiet. The only sound was the coffee machine, rumbling quietly, like a heart beating in the distance. Inside, it was as if the hush had intensified everything. Even as I turned the page of my magazine, the sound of the paper appeared to cut loudly through the air.

There was an indefinable chill in the café, as if an unexpected breeze had suddenly entered through the door and never left. Something was mingling with the silence, into the very fabric of the place.

Tony's right foot was tapping the floor, thud, *thud*. Sarah started to fan her face again and a bored look crossed her face.

Davla went outside and cleared the empty crockery from a table and then hurried in. The sound of the cutlery and the plates being placed in the sink echoed right back to where we sat.

I walked over to the counter, eager to break whatever tension was descending upon us. I stood there for a few minutes, and Davla didn't notice me, I waited for her to finish. When she finally turned around, she jumped.

'Nina, you really scared the hell out of me,' she squealed.

We faced each other awkwardly and then she smiled.

'It's been so crazy here today. Thankfully, it's quieter now, so I'll just take a break before someone else comes in,' she said.

She poured herself an orange juice and was about to head over to the table where I'd been sitting, when a man's voice behind us stopped her in her tracks.

'Any chance of a refreshing drink?'

Davla rolled her eyes at me.

We both turned around at the same time, and there standing in the open doorway, with a pile of books and papers in his hands, was James.

'This looks like a cosy gathering,' he muttered. He stepped in, placing his pile on the table nearest the door. Everyone looked at him as he smoothed his hair out and straightened his blue shirt.

'Can I quickly get a glass of ice cold water?' he asked Davla.

'I'm on my way to a seminar at the Bishopsgate Institute on the French existentialist writers, it's Camus today.'

'Sounds a bit too much for such a nice day,' Davla said. She left her juice on the table and came back with a glass of water, handing it to James.

Her mobile rang loudly and she frowned when she realised who it was.

'Excuse me James, it's my mother.'

She stepped into the doorway speaking rapidly in Portuguese.

James came over to me.

'Ever since I've been coming here, Davla's mother seems to be the thorn in her side. Oh dear, let's just hope today's not a bad one,' he said quietly.

'What are you two whispering about?' Sarah asked, coming up to us.

'Oh nothing, I'm just sorting my notes out. You know I like to be prepared,' James said.

'I suppose once a teacher, always a teacher. That's extremely organised of you. Are you looking for answers to the best of all possible worlds?' Sarah asked.

James stopped rifling through his papers and looked up at her in surprise.

'That's a different strand of philosophy,' he said, smiling. 'But I'm glad you've read up on some Martin Heidegger.'

'Leibniz actually,' Sarah said and James' face turned red. 'He was an eternal optimist and reckoned that God made the best of all possible worlds, it was his solution to the problem of evil.'

'Yes, well, very good, that was my next guess.'

'How do you see the world James? Is it a half empty glass or half full?' she asked.

This is an interesting way to pass my time.

I heard James' thought echo close to me. It was the same thing that had happened with Tony. I wondered if I was going mad.

***

'Perhaps you were tired, extremely tired. I'm surprised nobody else could hear, Nina,' Pieter said softly.

'I swear I heard it,' I said. 'Let me explain.'

***

'Sarah, I mostly see the glass half full,' James said. 'Look, I'd love to debate with you all afternoon, I honestly would, but I must be going. By the way, you should read up on Heidegger's *Being and Time*. I think you'll understand the bits about human existence passing through angst and mortality.'

'Goodness, it sounds like he's writing about my marriage.' Sarah laughed and James smiled sympathetically.

'That'll be you and the masses, my dear,' he said.

Suddenly, he straightened his books and swept everything up in his arms, as he headed for the door. I noticed that his hair had been trimmed and looked neater.

'Ciao, folks,' James said. 'We should all go out sometime.'

He squeezed past Davla and blew her a kiss. Sarah and I stood watching his haphazard exit, clutching his books and papers like the fictional Professor Branestawm. He almost collided with a woman on a bike coming from the opposite direction.

I returned to reading my magazine and after a few minutes, I saw Davla standing quietly, looking forlorn in the doorway. She had finished her phone conversation and was smoking silently, lost in her thoughts.

Sarah and Tony talked amongst themselves. It was clear that Davla didn't want to join us, she was happy to stay there and watch the people walk past in the street. We sat there for a while, glancing at her occasionally, yet none of us disturbed her.

CHAPTER FIVE

Davla was not in a particularly good mood the next time I saw her. From the moment that I stepped into the café, I noticed her frowning before she'd even spotted me. She kissed me hastily on both cheeks, telling me how good it was to see me, but her indifference towards me indicated otherwise. Her face was strong and relentless, even the beautiful chiffon pink dress and silver metallic heeled shoes that she wore didn't soften her appearance.

All afternoon, she slammed empty plates and cups down on the counter, it was a wonder that nothing broke. I sipped my lemonade in silence, wondering what to say.

She sighed and suddenly threw the cloth onto the floor in frustration and sat down on the stool.

'What's happened?' I asked her.

'It's just the same shit every day,' she said. 'I'm always just cleaning, making sandwiches, a tourist needs directions blah blah. I'm a hamster on a wheel.'

It was another hot day and only a few people came to the café. Davla was holding an unlit cigarette delicately between her fingers. She looked like a movie starlet, posing for a photograph.

'What's it like living with James?' she asked suddenly.

'It's good, better than I thought it would be.'

'I really need to give up the smoking. So seriously, James hasn't hit on you, has he?' She put the cigarette back in her bag.

I looked at her, and we both laughed.

'Come on Davla! He isn't like that, he's a gentleman.'

'I had a thing for him for a while.' Davla smiled mischievously. 'I think he was flattered by the attention but he never did take it any further. He's too engrossed in his books.'

'His flat is like a library, have you ever been there?' I asked.

'I've never been invited,' Davla said.

***

'Maybe James thought he was a philosopher or something,' Pieter said. 'Like a contemporary Socrates, ready to talk to anyone who would listen. He sounds like a typical lonely old man.'

'Who knows? It seemed to me that James was still burying the hurt from his wife's death through all the talks he attended.'

'You mean he hadn't dealt with it?' Pieter asked.

'That's the impression I got from staying with him. He was a sensitive soul, a thinker you know?' I replied.

'Yes, but he was a Christian too, so he must have believed that she had gone to a better place? Like you do with your nan,' Pieter insisted.

'I think he wanted to believe that,' I said. 'In reality though, he kept himself busy by reading and attending lectures and trying to forget her. It became a tug-of-war between his mind and his heart.'

***

In the café, Davla was staring at two guys walking past outside, laughing together. A sudden gush of air from the open door brought us relief from the heat.

'Jesus, it's so hot,' she said, jumping off the stool. 'I just want to go to a beach somewhere and jump in the sea to cool off.'

She disappeared around the back of the café, her heels clicking on the floor. When she came back, she gave me another glass of lemonade with crushed ice cubes full to the brim.

'On the house,' she said. She was standing so close that I could see the movement in the streets reflected in her green eyes. Her gaze shifted towards the open café door, and I saw a tall African man walk inside.

Davla greeted him lavishly and offered him some of her fresh lemonade. The zesty smell of lemons filled the air and reminded me of the homemade lemonade I'd had with nan several times in Delhi.

'Nina, this is Eric, a good friend of mine. He also helps me run the café sometimes.'

Eric glanced at me quickly and smiled warmly. He was wearing a pale yellow shirt, and jeans turned up at the bottom, with green flip flops. He had a neatly trimmed goatee beard and medium length dreadlocks tied back. His dark handsome face was slightly pockmarked.

He wore a necklace carved in wood with intricate rhinos, elephants, giraffes and a hippo.

'I thought I'd surprise you and so I left work early, babe. Has it been busy?' He asked looking around.

'Not really, just a handful,' she said.

'A good handful, I hope. You're just having a bad day that's all, love. Well, you're looking good anyway,' Eric said, and he winked at me.

Davla smiled and turned to serve a group of tourists who had just stepped in.

'So, you're the new face at the café. Davla mentioned you. Welcome to the jungle.'

With Eric's arrival the café appeared brighter. Davla had turned the radio on and when she finished serving the tourists, a group from the theatre arrived and suddenly the place was full. The tables outside were snapped up in an instant.

'I just bring her good luck,' Eric said, laughing. 'By the way, I've heard you've moved in with James?'

'Word does get around here,' I muttered.

He laughed.

I told him how inquisitive James could be and how crowded his living room was.

'It seems to me that you can take his questions in two ways,' Eric explained. 'Either he's genuinely curious and has this huge quest for knowledge or he's just a plain nosy bastard.'

'It's probably a bit of both.'

'How long will you be staying there?' Eric asked.

'Until early Autumn. Then I was thinking about taking a job abroad, maybe in Europe,' I said.

'Where will you go?'

'I'm interested in Amsterdam.'

'I like that, you're aiming high,' Eric said, smiling.

I watched him as he placed tobacco on a rizla and licked his lips on the edge.

'Excuse me a mo.' He stepped outside and smoked it.

Davla was talking to a man from the theatre group.

I'm so tired of being polite to you, asshole. And of this place sapping my energy.

Her thoughts came across to me like a radio frequency. I could see that there was a special energy in the café and I was being guided to another level of awareness, one far deeper than I'd ever experienced. I could see what people were really thinking and in Davla's case she was exhausted. This intrusion into peoples' lives was embarrassing, but also enlightening. I had no idea how it was happening and it made me feel a bit dizzy. The bottom of Davla's dress fluttered slightly and I saw her shiver too as if an invisible force had passed through her.

***

'Is it possible she actually said that to you?' Pieter asked. 'No one can read someone else's thoughts, that can't be true.'

'That's what happened,' I said, a little sharply. 'So, let me carry on with my story.'

***

Eric came back in.

I told him that I liked his necklace; up close it was beautiful.

'It's from Kenya, where I'm from,' Eric explained. He told me that his relatives lived in a village near Lake Victoria.

With the evening beginning to descend, it became fresher outside. Davla disappeared around the back of the café and turned the radio off. She came back and lit the candle on the table next to us. The flame flickered and its shadow danced on the wall. Davla was leaning forward and her face glowed from the flame.

'You know Nina I didn't expect you to come back to this café after your first visit, I'm really surprised you did,' she said.

'Darling, you're hardly selling the place with that speech,' Eric said loudly and she pulled a face at him.

'This is a unique place,' I said without a moment's hesitation.

'I feel it's my destiny to understand something here. You see, I lost my nan to cancer a short while ago and even before then, I'd been looking for something in life far deeper than I was used to.'

'And you think this place will help?' Davla asked, laughing. 'Do you want a full tarot reading, is that what you mean?'

'You've already given me a quick reading and it's confirmed what I now know to be true. That I am searching for happiness. Yes, that's what it is, you said I was on a journey, right?

'It's true, I am. I couldn't have put it better myself. I need to know that the shallow people I've been with, the fighting I saw with my parents, the death of my beautiful nan isn't the end of life. My obsession with my job, becoming successful, was all I gave a damn about and I needed something else. So, my discussion with James about God made me think about what happens afterwards, what you decide, well, that's your choice. All my friends cast labels such as *new* age on things they don't understand, but it's far too bloody easy to do that. I really need to *know* there's more to life, that's all.'

'Wow, I wasn't expecting that.' Davla looked shocked. 'You're on a mission that's for sure, girl. Let's hope it's not mission impossible. Why not just go to church, like James? Won't that help?'

'That would make her more confused,' Eric said, laughing gently.

***

I was surprised at the rush of emotions that came out from somewhere deep inside me and for a second I felt I was back at the Ganges again.

'Ashes to ashes, dust to dust,' mum had whispered to herself, not realising that I had heard her.

***

'I couldn't live with James myself, he's a lovely man, don't get me wrong. It's just when he preaches in here, people leave the café,' Davla said, interrupting my thoughts.

'What does he preach?' I asked.

'It's just that he thinks he knows everything about life and that really gets on my nerves because we all know a little something. Last week there was a couple having lunch in here and James started talking about God being external and internal to them and at first they thought he was interesting. Then he said man had to bring the external and internal elements together and the couple just looked confused and in the end I had to break up the little party and asked James to calm down, before the guy hit him.'

Eric laughed. 'James is cool, man. He's just a little lonely that's all.'

'We're all a little lonely,' Davla said loudly. 'It's just sometimes you've got to recognise when to stop. I mean I believe in energy out there, call it God. The image of God I was raised with was one of a strict old man with a long beard pointing his big stick at me whenever I had any fun, especially any sex.'

'James will only drive himself crazy if he keeps on acting like that,' Eric said. 'I think he needs another woman, a good woman.'

'He's obsessed with his wife.' Davla sighed. 'I doubt he'll ever get another woman.'

Nobody came into the café, and sometime later Davla opened a bottle of shiraz for us. Eric turned back to me and raised his glass.

'Cheers,' he said, and we all clinked glasses.

'What are we celebrating?' Davla asked.

'We're celebrating friendship and that Nina has found this place. I hope it does change your life for the best,' Eric said gently.

Davla's mobile rang shrilly, breaking the peaceful atmosphere. She rushed to the counter to answer it. She stood by the door speaking loudly in Portuguese.

'It's her family again. They're constantly calling her. Davla just ignores the phone sometimes.'

'Why do they ring so often?'

He shrugged. 'I think they just worry, especially her dad.'

Davla stepped outside and she was on the phone for a long time.

The candle-holder cast a gold circular glow on the table.

'It's difficult trying to find where any of us is heading sometimes,' Eric suddenly said. He was looking at me curiously, yet his face was unreadable.

'Yes, it's a lonely journey but this wine is helping.'

'Let it temporarily stop that brain thinking, thinking,' he said, grinning and pointing at my head.

'I'm really starting to think I was meant to come to here, although I'm not entirely sure why,' I told him.

'Well, it is an extraordinary place.'

'Why do you say that?'

'There's a good energy here that you can learn from, I'm sure you can feel that already?'

'Yes, I can, definitely.' I gulped down too much wine.

'It's like good spirits watching over, trying to guide you in here,' Eric said.

'Do you believe that people who pass over can do that?' I asked.

'Why not, people believe in angels and demons, don't they? Angels are supposed to help us, so why can't people who once loved us, who have now died?' he asked.

Nan's face flashed before my mind. I must have looked sad, because Eric touched my hand lightly and I looked up at him.

'I'm sure you'll know what to do next,' he said quietly. 'For God's sake, you can't spend the rest of your days coming here. You might go mad.' He had a lovely smile.

***

'I'll agree with Eric there,' Pieter said, interrupting me. 'It's like in your grief, you really imagined a lot of things. I'm not sure if your tale is one of fantasy or fact right now.'

'I wasn't imagining it,' I said, quietly. I felt sadness cloud me. 'Do you want me to continue Pieter, because your scepticism is affecting me, I have to admit.'

Pieter grabbed my hand.

'Continue, please.' He nodded. 'If this ends with us breaking up, so be it.'

I glared at him.

'It's a joke Nina, just go on, I'm all ears,' he laughed.

'Ok, so I was explaining about the conversation between me and Eric.' I felt uneasy but I carried on.

***

'I think it's good I'm here right now, it's helping me find my feet,' I told Eric.

'And that's important. But once you've found them, start running and never look back,' he said.

'Where are you from in Kenya?' I asked him.

'From a village called Kisumu. I used to swim and fish a lot of the time, with my friends. I swam with the hippos too and it never scared me. I didn't get *too* close, of course.

'In Kenya, my life was full of people from everywhere, young and old alike. I had so many friends when I was twelve and most of them were in their twenties and thirties.'

'It sounds idyllic.'

'It really was. All my family are over there, I'm here alone. My grandmother lives with us and she just turned a hundred!'

'Are you serious?'

'Of course, she lived a peaceful life, that's why.'

'That's incredible,' I said.

Eric shrugged. 'Everything seems incredible until it happens,' he said, asking me how old nan was when she died.

'She was seventy-eight,' I said and I realised that my voice was trembling slightly.

He nodded and before I could stop myself, I found myself telling him that I missed her greatly, and that I hadn't realised how much her death would affect me. The visits to nan in India had been like a safe haven to return to. They had been multi-layered with depth and emotion. Her presence had been a solid rock, filled with love. She had also imparted her spiritual values to me, as stories and sayings from what she knew and read. The seeds of those values were felt when I was young. Yet it was only now after her death, that they resonated with me. I was now beginning to cultivate them.

'Death is a mystery, babe,' Eric said. 'It's like a hard slap in the face.'

I nodded. I sensed that I could trust him completely, and that despite his closeness to Davla, he was not about to tell her anything about our conversation.

Suddenly Davla rushed back in, her heels slamming furiously on the floor. She glanced at us and I saw that her eyes were red.

'What happened?' Eric asked.

'That was my sister on the phone. A close family friend, Lucy, has just died of a heart attack, shit, only half an hour ago. I can't believe it. My mother is in shock as we've known her since we moved to London, but mum still managed to tell me off for not coming to visit this week.'

Her eyes filled with tears and Eric went over to her and put his arm around her.

'I think my mother can be cruel sometimes. Lucy was like an older sister to me,' Davla sobbed.

Mother is so selfish. She always acts as if she knows what's best for me, yet she doesn't even know me. She hasn't seen my heart.

Davla's thought at that moment came to me like an arrow and with my new found awareness, it made me sad.

I was sure that nan was reaching out to me from another world. I felt she wanted me to understand everything she had tried to teach me when I'd been with her. She wanted me to see beyond what most people saw as the physical reality they lived in. I wasn't afraid anymore of hearing these thoughts, and I was realising fast that people had several layers to them. The café was stripping the superficial layers away, so that they were vanishing and the reality was becoming clear to me.

My phone rang and I answered it quickly as Eric and Davla spoke in whispers to each other.

It was James.

'I'm making a magnificent roast dinner and thought you might like to join me.' He sounded cheerful.

'I'd like that, thanks James. I'll be back shortly.'

Eric and Davla were both looking at me when I hung up.

***

'So, he made fancy dinner for you too?' Pieter asked, enviously. 'I definitely think he had a crush on you, don't you honey?'

'It was only dinner, nothing special,' I said hastily.

'I believe you. I'm only winding you up,' he said, yet he looked serious.

***

In the café, Eric gave me a quick kiss on my cheek.

'Thanks for coming, Nina. No doubt I'll see you soon,' Davla said, still upset. She hurriedly hugged me and closed the door.

I was about to cross the street when it started to pour. Fat raindrops fell thick and fast, the sky thundered and lightning followed quickly.

I didn't have my umbrella and I considered running back inside the café again. The canopy outside was waving fiercely in the wind and a crushed can scuttled near a drain. It seemed like I was the only one on the street.

Through the window of the café, I could see Davla and Eric close together, two dark silhouettes huddling. Eric had pulled Davla close to him and her head rested on his shoulder.

It looked like Davla was crying, I wasn't sure. They weren't looking out of the window, only at each other so they didn't see me. Their faces were close to each other and as I watched, Davla kissed Eric swiftly on his lips. The touch of their lips was fleeting, like the fluttering wing of a butterfly.

Eric's lips met for a second with Davla's and the dainty kiss it brought forth was the flight of the butterfly, as it struggled to leave its mark on the world. If I hadn't looked through the window at that moment, I would never have seen it.

I arrived home soaked, feeling chilled to the bone. James took pity on me and made me a cup of warm herbal tea, after telling me how stupid I was for not staying in the café through the worst of the storm.

As he served dinner, the television was on and the weatherman was saying that it was the first of the summer storms. That night the rain fell hard and fast for a long time.

CHAPTER SIX

'What do you know about Rasputin?' James asked me early the next morning, as he poured me a cup of tea.

'Not much.' I yawned and reached for a slice of toast.

He had already showered and was whistling *New York New York.*

'I slept well yesterday in spite of that blasted rain. Anyway, you can't tell it's been pouring, can you?' he said, looking out of the window as the sun filtered in.

He was dressed in a crisp dark blue shirt which was complimented by khaki trousers. A hint of aftershave lingered in the air.

'James, are you off somewhere special today?'

'Nothing as exciting as that, I'm afraid. I've been invited to a discussion about the Russian monarchy over at Westminster University. I wrote a paper about it last year and now it's been picked up by a professor of European history. He's invited me to discuss it with his first year students.'

'That's great, but I still don't know much about Rasputin,' I said.

'Well, then you won't know that the British government had a strong interest in killing him.'

'Why was that?'

His eyes lit up as he started speaking, as if my interest had rekindled his passion.

'Well, they wanted him dead because he was against Russia's intervention in the First World War and look what happened there! The Germans defeated them and then after that, most of the Russian monarchy was slaughtered by the Communists. What a way to go.

'There were all kinds of attempts to finish off Rasputin, but he kept surviving and the Tsars' wife wouldn't hear a bad word against him. Can you imagine four attempts on his life and he still carries on, what should we make of that?'

'Perhaps he just wasn't supposed to die?' I suggested.

'Exactly, his destiny was to stay alive and God let him. I can only conclude that was for a purpose.'

'What purpose?'

'To be honest with you dear, if I knew the answer I would be God, don't you think? And I'm not God. I am a mere mortal like you.'

He laughed heartily and I realised that he must have been a passionate teacher.

I left him for a moment and when I came back, James was sitting behind his desk, his head bent low and his glasses pushed up on his forehead. He was scribbling furiously on his notebook and I saw the page filling up rapidly with his words. They were written in black and I saw that he was using a fine ink pen. I imagined it to be a quill, used by writers in medieval times and before, to write and sign their manuscripts. I wondered what he was writing about – a new theory or debate. Whatever it was, he was engrossed in his work.

James let the ink on the page dry for a minute and then gently turned the pages of the notebook. He lifted the cracked leather cover and then put it down again. I hardly dared to breathe in case he caught me secretly observing him. I imagined he was caught up in his theories, like the ancient philosophers I had come across as a student.

I saw him akin to the world of Plato and his great pupil Socrates to Soren Kierkegaard and Descartes and his philosophy: *I think therefore I am*. In his time, men believed in reason and the rational mind and I remembered the endless debates at University about Socrates and the immortality of the soul, about Soren Kierkegaard and existentialism and the leap of faith towards God. These men had endeavoured to impart their ideas to the masses and leave their mark on mankind, just like James was leaving an impression on me now.

I must have stood there for a few minutes watching his hands move deftly across the paper. It appeared that he was intent on placing his thoughts down rapidly before they deserted him. At that moment, he seemed to me like a magnificent philosopher.

Suddenly James stopped writing. He appeared spooked as if a ghost had just tapped him on the shoulder. He looked up slowly in the direction of where I stood and his eyes focused on mine sharply.

'Nina, for heavens sake! *What in God's name are you doing?*'

My voice stuck in my throat.

'Are you spying on me?' He laughed.

'I… I'm sorry.'

He stared at me for a while longer, his pen poised in mid air.

'If you're going to come in, then do. Don't just stand there like a lemon, watching me write. I can't think of a more boring way for you to pass your time.'

I stepped into the room, feeling embarrassed and sat down on the sofa. He was watching me, his face full of amusement.

'How long were you standing there?'

'Five minutes.'

He raised his eyebrows.

'Ok, ten, I think. What were you writing about? You seemed so engrossed.'

'I was finishing off my notes for this Russian monarchy lesson. It all comes back to me once I start writing like that.'

***

'I can't believe you really thought James was a philosopher,' Pieter said, turning to me suddenly and surprising me with his interruption. 'You seem really infatuated with him.'

'I wasn't infatuated, more interested in his ideas, he was a wealth of knowledge and I knew I could learn a lot from him. I never knew you had this streak of jealousy in you, Pieter. You seem to be annoyed with James for no reason.'

'I'm not jealous,' Pieter said. 'Just tired, darling. Anyway, tell me more as I have to admit James does intrigue me.'

***

'We are all teachers you know,' James remarked quietly to me. 'I am flattered that you've been comparing me to the great Socrates.' He laughed again and then became thoughtful.

'Funny, my wife used to say the same thing. She told me I was like a philosopher and I always had something to say, usually something that didn't make a lot of sense.'

His eyes wandered around the room and stopped on the photograph of him with Angela in Istanbul.

'All these pictures keep reminding me of her. Seeing what she went through in those last days, those final hours were agony. When the hospital called to tell me she was getting worse, I drove there like a madman. I knew Angie was going to die, I just knew. My dear, the back end of life is such a bastard.'

He looked sad as he continued.

'I felt angry, as if something was going to happen beyond my control. It was a Saturday and I was feeling very low. I was here, alone, praying in the morning, desperately asking God to show me a sign that she would be OK, but I knew she wouldn't make it.

'I reached the Chelsea and Westminster hospital and she was so weak, that I could only hold her hand and talk to her and it was a different kind of talk, deeper than any we'd ever had. She thanked me for the happiest days of her life and expressed her sadness for not having had children. She felt guilty for leaving me alone, I think.'

I thought of nan and the tears came to my eyes unexpectedly. I remembered how inconsolable my mother had been for days after she had passed away.

'You know Angie sat right where you are my dear, just a few years ago. She said her head hurt and her body felt like it was on fire, after another chemo session.'

His words were rushed and uneasily spoken, running into each other like dominoes toppling one after another.

'I'm sorry, James, that sounds like a horrible experience,' I said.

***

'How did his experience make you feel?' Pieter asked me. 'You've never shared the depth of this with me before.' He sounded desolate.

I wanted to hug him but I hesitated. 'I missed nan and all the little details I'd forgotten about her, suddenly came back to me,' I said.

'You know the freckles across her nose, the sound of her voice. Hearing James made me miss her terribly. Yet at the same time, in a strange way it was comforting to know someone else had gone through the same pain.'

***

James' voice came back to me.

'That last Sunday I went to see Angie at the hospital and she was still alive and my hopes lifted and I went to get a coffee. When I came back, she was gone, just like that. Like a flame that burns brightly for a second and when your back is turned, it's no longer there,' James continued.

He stood up from his desk and picked up a photograph lying beneath the others on the mantelpiece. It was of two Sufi dancers in Turkey. They were dancing with their arms outstretched. Their attire was all white, including a hat and long tunics. One dancer's arm was outstretched towards the ceiling, the other towards the ground.

'That was the night we saw the whirling dervishes. The dance is supposed to symbolize a communion with God and it meant a lot to us because Angie had just finished her chemo treatment and was given the all clear by the doctors. We didn't know she'd get sick again two years later.'

He excused himself and disappeared into the hallway. When he came back, he was wearing the robe like the whirling dervishes.

'James, that really looks good on you. Did they give that to you?'

'They did actually, isn't it great? We made friends with Ali, one of the dancers, and he invited us to dinner with his family the next day.

When we explained why we'd come to Turkey and Angie's illness, he gave me the tunic as a gift. I came back and took some lessons in Sufi dancing before life became too busy. You'll have to watch it without the music though.'

He stood up and I could see his bare feet sticking out, the tight white trousers over his tunic appeared too long for him. He stretched out his arms as he had practised, slightly self-consciously. His face was composed, yet he looked lonely.

A man's life is in his hands. I thought of nan.

He was looking up now past me to my left, close to the window. He seemed to have forgotten I was there; he was totally absorbed in the moment. I felt the sincerity of what he was doing and I was transfixed by it.

He began to dance, awkwardly at first, then gaining confidence. He lifted his arms and turned faster and faster. His tunic swayed furiously, rising up and swinging around with a whoosh, his large feet turned on the same spot.

He was so composed that I couldn't quite believe he could do it.

It was as if he were looking beyond my presence, as if he'd transcended the room completely. He was concentrating hard and as he continued to turn in rhythm, his feet and arms moved gracefully. He seemed to me to be the happiest I'd ever seen him, carefree in his dance, joining his union with God.

He was in the middle of another turn, when a gust of wind from the open window whipped up the tunic and it fluttered, as if there was an invisible fan underneath.

The movement of the cloth as it flirted with the wind was gentle like a balloon drifting out to sea, floating on an extraordinary force. That force was like a river flowing so fast that it washed away everything in its path. It crashed against the rocks on its journey, yet it sustained and carried everything with a mighty energy. I thought it was like life itself, fragile and yet fierce too.

It was delicate, and in my imagination I saw a butterfly near James' tunic as he turned in his dance. Its wings went up and down fluttering like the tunic.

'James, that's really fantastic,' I said.

'What are you thinking of now?' James asked breathlessly. He was sitting down again. 'Are you off into Neverland again?'

I laughed and he stood up and smiled at me.

'Don't you need to enlighten students about the Russian monarchy?' I asked.

'I'm off to change now. It's been a pleasure my dear! I never thought I'd be wearing this again, I can tell you!'

With that he made his way to his room, his tunic making him appear like a ghost as he walked out into the hallway.

CHAPTER SEVEN

As I crossed Shaftesbury Avenue and entered Soho early the next morning, I remembered the vivid images of the gold bangles nan used to wear, designed for her by my uncle. I recalled the way she would gently touch my arm to get my attention. Those images pierced my thoughts and I felt the force of emotion again inside.

It was early and warm already.

Davla looked up as I entered the café. She was sitting alone at a table with a cup of coffee, doing her bookwork. She appeared vibrant in her emerald silk shirt and tight jeans.

'Morning, Nina, you're earlier than usual. Have you fallen out with James?' she asked curiously, getting up to pour me a cup of fresh coffee.

'Actually, I was out before him, just for a change. I've decided to look at my next career move.'

'Ah, I see, so that kept you awake all night? Well, feel free, I'm flattered that you think you can work here,' she laughed.

The café was an oasis of calm. The place had been cleaned. The mirrors were gleaming, the windows were clear as glass and the tables reflected light. The books had all been arranged neatly on the shelves.

Davla continued with her book work, entering numbers furiously on her calculator.

'You know days like this, when it's so peaceful, that's when I miss home. It's always lively in Brazil. When I wake up there, the sun is always shining,' Davla said.

'You must have been to the carnival several times,' I said.

'Of course I have. What you have to understand about Brazil is that there is so much poverty there and Brazilians wouldn't have a chance of surviving without their energy and creativity. So, the carnival is not just a way of life, it's a necessity.'

She put her calculator down.

'I think after this summer, I'll be making plans to move back to Sao Paulo. I've been getting itchy feet, as you English say, is that right?'

'You're feeling restless?' I asked.

'In Portuguese, we have this saying: *saudade*. It's like a yearning of the soul or homesickness. I feel like that today.'

'What about Brazilian men, they're sexy aren't they?' I asked.

'And that's on your mind, first thing?' Davla asked and she smiled at my digression. 'In my experience they are too macho.'

She stood up, stretching her arms. I could see that she was wearing her silver metallic shoes.

'You know the scariest thing is that sometimes I feel as if I am connected to this place and no matter how hard I try, I just can't break free,' she said.

'I'm sure it's not forever.'

'True, nothing's forever, but that's not reassuring, Nina.'

'I like this place,' I said, and she looked at me questioningly. 'If I hadn't come here, I wouldn't have met you or James.'

'That's very sweet and I suppose you have found a place to live by coming here,.' she remarked.

She looked in one of the mirrors and fiddled with her hair. *Sometimes, I really don't like what I see*. I heard a whisper, nothing more.

She turned back to her calculator and idly typed something in, swearing when it made an error.

'This thing is useless. I can't believe that I've actually made a profit this month. I've checked this four times now, the calculator can't be wrong every time.'

'Don't you have an accountant who takes care of all that?'

'Usually it's Eric, he's terrific with figures. He's been keeping my records for a few months now. He's got quite a brain on that gorgeous head of his.'

***

I stopped my story and turned to Pieter.

'That's when I called you. I remember because you had just texted me and Davla was complaining about the calculator.'

'Oh yes, our first flirty text, I told you that I'd liked meeting you and I thought you had lovely eyes,' Pieter said. It was darker now and the street was busy with the evening crowds heading to the bars and theatres. The café was shrouded in darkness and I could see nothing inside. It was in stark contrast to how it had been that day when I'd been talking to Davla.

'I was so pleased when I got that message from you. I sent you a text straight away and later you called me,' I said.

I had first met Pieter at a bar in the City. My close girlfriends Nicola and Sam had invited me out. I didn't want to go but they'd insisted, as they wanted to cheer me up after nans' death.

As the bar was crowded, we had to share a long table with a group of bankers from Europe and one of them was Pieter.

Nicola started to chat to the man sitting next to her, while Sam bought the next round of drinks and I went outside to answer a call from my mother.

By the time I came back, there was a lively debate going on with Nicola, Sam and two of the men. I noticed another man sitting next to Nicola and I liked the way his dimples appeared on his cheeks when he smiled. He was laughing with the others but appeared too shy to join in the conversation.

'Yes, I remember that there was an instant attraction and I couldn't forget you when I went back to Amsterdam,' Pieter said, looking intently at me now.

'Did you find me attractive? I thought I looked depressed that day,' I said.

'You were quiet but once we started chatting, I liked you straight away,' Pieter said.

'Me too, that's why I gave you my number. Davla's sharp ears didn't miss a thing either,' I said and I returned to my story.

***

'Pieter?' Davla asked, after I'd hung up. 'Who's that, a new love in your life?'

'Oh, just this Dutch guy I met recently.'

'Hopefully something will happen with Pieter,' Davla said. 'Whenever I'm looking for a man, nothing happens. It's only when I don't look that I meet them.' She laughed.

'Come on Davla, men are always falling at your feet. Sometimes I think they come in the café only because they spot you first.'

She seemed pleased by my comment and was now in the mood to talk more.

'My family arrived in Brazil as Portuguese immigrants and lived in Curitiba, a city in the South. My father was a wealthy businessman importing and exporting goods from Europe and my mother was a teacher. We moved to Sao Paulo when I was twelve and I'm really glad we did because we lived there until I was eighteen and I really loved it,' she said.

The memory of that time came back to her and in the café, her memories came to life again.

'I suppose you can say I was a wild teenager, my mother didn't know what to do with me. I went to parties and took drugs. I thought I was in control of my life then, when really I was so lonely.'

She looked around to make sure no one came in and then looked at me.

'It's funny but since you've come to this café, you've brought an element of good luck with you. I'm getting more customers for my tarot readings, more people are coming in and Eric and James really like you. I feel I can trust you, Nina. You're like a nomad who wandered in here and helped us all,' she said.

I was surprised to hear her say that.

'I've been doing well here, but I've been praying to get back home. You don't know how sad I've been for so many months. I've been asking God, and yes I do believe in *something* still, to see me through in these days of darkness.'

'Has it been that bad?'

'Yes, it's been hard. You see, when I was younger I loved God, I went to church with my mother in Sao Paulo until I was thirteen and then I didn't care anymore.'

'What happened?' I asked.

'The relationship between my mother and I changed as I became a young woman. She'd always been reluctant to show her love for me, now she just criticised everything. My hair, the clothes I bought, the way I spoke. It was like she was trying to break me down and then mould me as she wanted me to be. I asked God to show me what was happening but he was silent. I felt betrayed, so I stopped going to church and turned to men instead. You know when I lost my virginity? It was when I was fourteen and to a twenty-six year old. Let me just say that I felt older than my age, as if I were twenty.

'Sometimes we never used condoms and then I'd fret that I was pregnant. Amazingly, I never was and then I'd pray and thank God. I believe God protected me during that turbulent time. The man was the brother of a friend of mine from school and his name was Torben.'

She looked at me to see if her confessions were unsettling me.

'Didn't your parents find out?' I asked.

'No, but my older sister came home early from work once when my parents were away for the weekend. She saw us leaving the house and she threatened to tell my mother. You see my family were very strict and if my parents had found out that I'd been with this guy, all hell would have broken loose. I promised not to see him, but I didn't keep my word. I was crazy, he got me onto coke and I felt so powerful then, as if I were a goddess. Then one day, he left. No reason, nothing. I heard his family had moved away to Rio. He never contacted me again and after that, my family life was never quite the same. What about yours?' she asked me abruptly.

'As an only child during my teens, I had no reason to rebel,' I said and Davla nodded. 'My parents were proud of my A grades but after my degree, things changed.'

She looked at my expectantly.

'My family life started falling apart, I suppose the signs had always been there. My father was always a moody man ever since I could remember, so many weekends had been spent alone with my mother, helping her cook and doing my homework. I never knew where he was, I assumed it was business. I wasn't allowed out often with my friends, so I witnessed my mum's loneliness. Once we set a place for my father at dinner, but he didn't come home. I realised mum was crying quietly as she ate her potatoes and I went over to hug her and she pushed me away. That was the first realisation that something was really wrong.'

'Was there anyone you could talk to?' Davla asked.

'I wanted to talk to nan, but it would have worried her. So, I kept it to myself and later I asked my father why he wasn't around and he told me to stay out of things that didn't concern me.' My voice trembled slightly.

'Oh honey, he sounds horrible. Do you think he was having an affair?' Davla said.

'You don't know how many times I've asked that. Yes, I think he was, maybe even more than one. I called him a dirty bastard to his face once when I heard him talking to a woman on the phone, telling her he missed her. He became angry and was about to hit me when my mother walked in and he hit her hard instead and her nose started bleeding. I stood there stunned. It was as if the world had stopped for a few seconds. I snapped out of my spell, rushing to the bathroom to get some tissue paper. By the time I came back, she was slumped on the sofa. Blood ran from her nose onto her cream dress, splashing it with crimson spots. I was shaking as I handed her the tissues. I made her a cup of tea and she drank it slowly, gripping the cup as if her life depended on it. I locked the front door because I'd heard him slam it as he left and we didn't see him again until two days later.'

'Jesus Christ,' Davla said. 'What an animal! How was your mother, did she talk to you?'

'I wanted to call the police and she begged me not to do it. She said she loved him and she didn't want the police to know. I argued with her and she kept telling me to stop. In the end, she started crying hysterically and I comforted her but I felt angry. Her timidity and sense of worthlessness were so clear. I felt she was being a dumb Indian woman. The next morning, I called nan and had a long chat with her. I wanted to hear her voice and I needed the strength it gave me.'

***

'Wait a minute, wait a minute,' Pieter said loudly and the couple at the next table turned to look at us. The wine had taken his inhibitions away now. 'How come you've never told me this? Your dad was a wife beater? I mean, bang goes my theory of your idyllic little family.'

'Shush, be quiet,' I said, grabbing his arm and then letting go as he glared at me. 'I didn't think it was important.'

'Important?' he snapped. 'We've only been married five years!'

'Sorry,' I muttered. Pieter stared at me for a long, tense moment.

'Just carry on, I wonder what other surprises await me,' he said. His voice was edgy, fearful, full of anticipation.

***

'Nina, I'm so sorry, that's dreadful. So, your mother is Indian and your father?' Davla asked me.

'His family are from the Midlands. Davla, I don't want to depress you with my story.'

'You're not, did you tell your grandmother?'

'Not straight away, life at home became lonely and I closed off from my mother. I had just turned twenty-two and shortly afterwards, I convinced her that I needed to go to India. She seemed relieved that

I'd asked, as if she knew that we needed to be apart. So, I flew to Delhi on my own and had the most beautiful time with nan, visiting relatives and seeing the Taj Mahal. I still worried about my mother so I eventually told nan. My announcement made her cry and then she told me off for not telling her earlier. I wished I hadn't said anything as she wanted to call my mother immediately. She kept wringing her hands and her face was etched with worry. Luckily, she calmed down enough to listen to me and didn't call her or my uncles, as they would have come to London and finished off my father.'

'It sounds to me like he could have done with a good beating,' Davla said, sighing. 'My family look like the Waltons in comparison.'

'She was a wise woman, my nan. She called my mother every day and asked how she was and if she could visit soon. My mother never told her in a lot of detail about the violence and my nan kept praying for her every morning until the smell of incense was like a heavy cloud in the air. What could she do, being a million miles away?'

Davla touched my arm gently.

'You must miss your grandmother terribly,' she said.

'More than anything, she was the only true friend I had. You know, after I came back, I threw myself into my work, I was determined to be brilliant in public relations. I worked my way up and freelanced for various companies. I made superficial friends, but never any who lasted. I had flings with several men, went to fantastic parties. This went on for about seven years and during that time, I'd visit nan regularly, sometimes with my family, mostly without.'

'You spent all your holidays visiting your grandmother?' Davla asked.

'Not all, but most. We'd stand on her roof at her house in Delhi and discuss everything under the sun. Politics, friendships, my parents, the world, men, life and death, there was nothing too big or too small.'

I felt the tears stinging my eyes as I spoke and Davla put her arm around me.

'Then the day comes when she just isn't there anymore and I am alone again.'

'We're all alone really aren't we?' Davla said quietly.

We were silent for a while afterwards and she returned to her accounts.

'Sometimes I'm afraid that if I stop for a second, life will pass me by. I'll see it sailing past and I'll be powerless to capture it and the speed of that will be astonishing. That's why I have to go back to Brazil,' Davla continued.

'It sounds like you've made your mind up,' I said.

'I have, it's just that my dad will be so disappointed. He's so proud to be working in London. He was offered a job in England when I was nineteen and it was a real culture shock coming here. My English was terrible and my jobs were rubbish. I was a waitress in Leicester Square, a bar maid in the city and an escort too for a while.'

'An escort?'

'I'm not ashamed to admit it, but don't you dare tell the others. At least I had money then although I had to sleep with guys who were ugly and smelt awful. I was known as the Brazilian kinky babe.' She laughed loudly. 'Until one Arab guy in Mayfair wanted me to take coke with him and it was like being with Torben. I couldn't get into that stuff again, it would have killed me.'

***

'So not only did you not tell me about your violent dad, but now it turns out that the café owner used to be a hooker?' Pieter asked me, looking incredulous. 'Excuse me for the interruption but I couldn't make this up if I tried. This café is turning out to be a crazy place.'

'The two are unrelated,' I said, coldly. 'Dad was violent, that's true and Davla only did it because she was desperate for money,' I said.

'I think that's why most women do it, honey,' Pieter said, sarcastically.

I felt like crying. If he saw my eyes welling up, he ignored it. I'd never seen this side of Pieter before. It was cold, detached, unsentimental. I thought I should stop and perhaps go back to the hotel. Yet it was my story, it involved my beloved nan and James and all the others from the wonderful café. I knew I couldn't stop, so I continued with my narrative.

***

'Those first few years in London were awful,' Davla told me. 'I wanted to go home and be with everything familiar. My mother and I became even more distant. Eventually we barely spoke. Things got so bad that I had to leave home and my dad helped me out financially. Then, on my twenty-ninth birthday, with his money and business advice, I opened this café. I didn't christen it or anything like that. It had no name because I wanted it to be unusual, branding wasn't important. It was, well, it was just *here*. Tell me honestly, Nina, what do you think of it?'

'I think it's a great place. It's quirky and peaceful and I feel my nan is here with me in spirit and I'm understanding more about life and people than I have ever before,' I said.

She looked at me as if she didn't quite believe me, her eyes searching mine.

'At least I've achieved something then.' She smiled and looked around the café, as if my words had made her see it differently.

'You know, I opened this little café two years ago already, we had a little party, popped open some champagne and everyone came to see me, even my mother.'

As the morning progressed, only a few customers came in.

Davla welcomed them as if she'd known them for years. It was as if she were awake for the first time in a long time to her feelings, she was cheerful and friendly. She served fresh lemonade that she had made herself and the smell of lemons gradually overtook the one of fresh coffee.

CHAPTER EIGHT

'Are you awake?' James was knocking lightly on my door. He was tapping a gentle rhythm that reached me as I lay in bed.

'It's gone eight and I've made some fresh tea my dear.'

I heard his footsteps as he walked away. The sun poured in through the window. I got up and opened it and the sounds of the morning rush hour filled the room.

James popped his head out of the living room door just as I was about to enter.

'Morning James, I'll be with you shortly.'

After I had showered and dressed, I went back to join him.

He was sitting on what I realised was his favourite spot now, the chair behind his desk, dressed smartly in a pinstriped black and white shirt tucked into cream cotton trousers.

He peered at me from over his newspaper with his glasses perched on the edge of his nose, gestured for me to sit down and poured me a cup of tea from the pot on the small table next to him.

'My talk on the Russian Revolution went down a treat, so I just watched telly yesterday. Are you settling in ok?' he asked, smiling and putting the paper down.

'I'm glad the talk was good and yes, I'm settling in fine.'

He looked pleased and then placed his cup, with the by now familiar words *world's favourite teacher*, onto the table next to him. The room seemed brighter than usual and he started reading his newspaper again.

'What are your plans for today?' I interrupted him.

'I'm going to play badminton with Tony and then I'll head for the café later. There might be some live music on too. You're welcome to join us later, my dear. I must say, you do keep yourself to yourself, rather a dark horse.'

'Am I?' I asked, a little defensively.

He laughed and told me to relax as he took a large gulp of tea.

'For a young lady, you can sometimes have a fiery side,' he said.

'Are you picking on me this morning?' I asked.

He said nothing and continued to read. Being in James' flat sometimes felt like being in James' mind and it was full of contradictions and complexities. I felt I was becoming part of the rise and fall of his thought processes.

I made myself some toast and asked James if he wanted some. He didn't respond, so I made extra ones.

He cut his toast into half diagonally and heaped strawberry jam on top, biting into it noisily.

He was in a pensive mood now. As he stood up, I became more aware of the books that he had opened yesterday. The presence of his books seemed to surround us like hungry birds.

The sun's rays brightened the wall behind us. James opened the window wider and looked out, placing his hands carefully on the window ledge. I could hear Beethoven's fifth symphony playing in a flat below as he looked out into the street.

I turned to go and James looked around swiftly.

'Leaving already?'

He walked back to his chair.

'I've got a lot to do,' I said, slinging my bag over my shoulder.

'Cheerio,' he said, not glancing up. 'Are you off to the café then? I'm afraid it doesn't open until later today, Davla has a funeral to go to.'

'Oh yes, her mother's friend, how did you know about that?'

'How did *you?*'

'I was in the café when her mother called.'

'Well, I spoke to Davla afterwards over the phone.'

'Oh, I see,' I said.

The bag fell like a stone off my shoulder as I stood in the doorway.

'Do come in and sit down if you want. She'll open at lunchtime and you can go then.'

I sat back down on the sofa.

'I had this conversation with Eric the other day and I told him that nowadays it's all about sex with young people. Very few bother to be friends anymore. After Angela and I got married, we were at it all the time for a while; don't get me wrong. Then, I suppose without realising it we became good friends.'

'James, you're not at Speakers' Corner now, you know?'

To my surprise, he laughed and told me that I was right.

'I suppose I am fond of moralising,' he said, as if he were proud of the fact.

'Just a little, aren't you going to be late for your badminton?'

'Probably but Tony's always late,' he said, chuckling.

'How did your wife put up with your theories and your moralising?' I asked, laughing.

He laughed too and then his face became sad again and I wished that I hadn't said anything.

'She put up with it because she loved me. Once we had a silly argument about nothing important. I can't even remember what started it. I do recall that it ended with the particulars of the Christian faith.

'I had staunchly defended the Protestant church that I went to. I had visited Angela's Catholic church three times already, more to please her than anything else. In all honesty, I found the sermons poorly presented and simplistic in their views, lacking any kind of purpose or direction.

'Undemanding *love thy neighbour* sermons did nothing for me. I found myself itching to elbow the priest out of the way and stand up in his place to talk to the congregation. Not because I wanted to particularly, at least not *that* congregation, but because I couldn't stand the boredom of it all. There was no spark in the speeches, to me they droned on like the hum of a plane, lacklustre and with no logical connections holding them together.'

'That does sound really boring,' I said, giggling.

'Oh, it was, I can tell you,' James replied. "If there's one thing I can't stand, it's words that don't follow each other beautifully, whether in a spoken sentence or written down. Nina, my mother told me when I was a young boy, that words were the jewels that lived inside a person. Do you believe that?'

'What did she mean?' I asked.

'She meant that everything a person says reflects who they are,' James explained. 'She told me that I'd get where I was going in life because of what I said to people. When I was twelve she told me off for shouting during dinner once. She'd said it with such clarity and calmness that I took notice and never forgot. When I became a teacher, I remembered to be patient whenever my students annoyed me.'

***

'My God, James really *was* a philosopher, wasn't he?' Pieter asked. 'If words meant so much to him, why didn't he become a speaker? Perhaps that would suit him. I mean he's either being deep with his words or he's just being bland.'

'It was interesting and I could see why he was a teacher,' I said.

'Oh, why was that?' Pieter seemed to be testing me.

'James thought that it was the beauty of words, written calmly in white chalk on a blackboard that presented a challenge to his students.'

'I think he was just eccentric,' Pieter continued. 'Does anyone in this day and age have time to reflect on what they are saying or reading? Why did he have this obsession with words?'

'James felt people didn't take the time to notice the beauty in what they were saying or reading anymore,' I said. 'He felt that we had no *feeling* in it now, or at least much less than we used to.'

Pieter nodded although I wasn't sure he understood me. He motioned with his hand for me to continue.

***

'Words are rather like a melody my dear, like Chopin would have played as his fingers flowed like water over the piano,' James said and he pretended to play a piano. He bent his fingers slightly as a pianist would; striking imaginary notes in the air.

'I think beautiful words, composed with awareness, are the beginning of a long conversation that are derived directly from the hand of God. When I was younger, I pored over pages of the work of Ludwig Wittgenstein, trying to get inside the head of a philosopher whom I felt understood me, a man who knew how important the essence of a word was.

'That's why, when I hear or read words that are poorly constructed in sentences that jump in all directions, like the sermons in Angela's church, I cringe for the whole nation,' James continued.

'You know, there was one particular priest, this fat bald man who was no orator and appeared never to have looked in or even heard of a thesaurus. He once talked about those who were poor in spirit, yet his own speech was so full of holes and mishaps, let alone terrible metaphors, that I felt I was hearing it from a five-year-old. Honestly Nina, that's how bad it was,' James said loudly.

'I wondered why he was talking about poverty, when the sermon was supposed to be about loving your neighbour as yourself. Angela had muttered *for goodness sake, can't you let it go?* But I couldn't, so I upset her by making several jibes about her Catholic background. It was just before we got married and it upset me, I was certain she'd end it! And in a way, I would have deserved that.'

***

'James sounds emotional, as if he was tired of being logical all the time,' Pieter said.

'Maybe you could take a leaf out of his book,' I replied, briskly.

'I prefer being myself, thanks,' Pieter said, fixing me with a stern look.

'Anyway, James' thoughts about his wife made me realise a lot about myself too,' I said. 'I was learning from him, I was questioning what I believed, was there a life after death and a God? None of these questions had mattered before but seeing James' passion and commitment for Angela, made me realise how I needed to live every moment with awareness so that I could treasure my memories with nan.'

'Words became alive in James and he used them as the foundation for everything, for his teaching, his debating and writing. They were the bricks upon which his house was built and that's why he had so many books. The problem was that since Angela's death words could no longer give him any comfort. They now failed him. And in that failing, he felt Angela's loss.'

'You mean he had built a wall around himself?' Pieter asked. 'Kind of like the Pink Floyd album, that's touching.'

'Pieter, stop teasing me,' I said. 'I guess it was similar. Those words of his became castles in the sand and they could not comfort him in his hour of need. It was like the voice of reason could not argue with the voice of pain. They were like boxers, facing each other in the ring. It was the voice of pain that overcame the voice of reason and destroyed the useless words, flattening their logical sequences. Angela's death was the single tragedy that had infiltrated his life so much.'

***

I remembered James went over to the window again, and he took a good look outside.

'The streets are really empty,' he said and it seemed like those words bore into him, like pressure rising in a well. I saw the expression on his face change, a look of pain crossed it.

'Sometimes, I can hear her voice Nina and I can recall our honeymoon over ten years ago.'

He let go off the windowsill, his eyes focused on something below. I wondered what he saw; he seemed to be looking *beyond* the street at something that I couldn't see.

'My love, it was wonderful, that's what Angie said and I remember those words now as if she has just shouted them to me again.'

'James, it's been four years. Shouldn't the pain have lessened by now?' I started to say.

'Time is irrelevant my dear, time only makes me feel her again. On certain days, she's back here by my side, whispering in my ear. Her delicate words are like droplets of the most precious rain, *jewels of a person*. She's still here, just like you feel your nan's presence.'

'Yes, I think she's with me often.'

'That's right, you see! So you do know what I mean. I feel Angela on another side in all her finery.'

'Tell me about a happy time with her, James.'

'With pleasure, I'll tell you about the happiest day of my life. It was the start of my honeymoon and we walked around Howth Head near Dublin.

'As we walked along close to the sea, I had my arm around Angie and I felt peaceful, happy even. She was wearing a lovely green dress.

'We passed the former home of the poet, William Butler Yeats. I had pointed that out excitedly, adding that the great poet had lived there when he was a young man, chasing moths and butterflies.

'We'd risen early for breakfast in the hotel near the centre of Dublin and then taken the train to Howth Head.

'I had already been there a few times before with my family, but never with a lover, and never with my wife. I was eager to please that day. I glanced at her constantly as we walked along because I loved the way she looked in that emerald dress. The contrast of that colour and the blue of the harbour were striking, and as we walked, I felt a wonderful harmony descend on us.

'Later, back at the hotel, I asked her how she felt about the day and I can still remember her words. *My love, it was wonderful,* she'd said.

'Now the poignancy of her words turn against me. They are like whispers thrown into the air coming to trouble me from time to time. They echo in my mind like constant chatter coming to disturb me.

'Those pleasures of peace are missing from my life now. I've never felt that way winning an argument at Speaker's Corner and those feelings of elation have long since deserted me. In the barrenness of my heart, my longing for my wife is still strong and I don't know if it will ever leave.'

'James,' I interrupted him, and he turned from the window and looked at me, emerging from the sea of another realm.

'That's beautiful, really it is. Do you think we should be making a move though?'

I saw that he was not really listening to me.

***

'I've heard about people not getting over the death of loved ones,' Pieter said. 'This is a bit too much, all this wallowing and self-pity. God, I think I need another drink.' He seemed tipsy already as he ordered a whiskey for himself and a coke for me.

'Pieter, he was an older man and he lost his wife,' I said, crossly.

'I know, I know,' Pieter said. 'And he was lonely as hell, it seems, poor guy.'

My mind turned to James again.

***

'On the last day of our honeymoon, we had dinner in a wonderful seafood restaurant with a woman in a glamorous sequinned black dress playing the piano. She was a local singer it turned out. She played *Cockles and Mussels* and I sang along, much to the amusement of everyone,' James said, laughing.

'You've got a good memory James,' I said.

'Oh yes, I remember everything that I said to her, word for word and now I am telling you, my dear. There it is, a string of words, linked like a row of origami shapes, springing from the depths of my memory into the midst of your world now.'

For a long time neither of us spoke.

'You know Nina, just when I think everything is grounded again in my life, Angie finds her way back into my world,' James said.

'Or is it you who finds your way into hers?' I asked.

He looked at me as if I'd just slapped him in the face.

'Didn't you say you had to go?' he sounded vulnerable.

I wanted to tell him that I understood. I knew because of my despair at nan's loss. James had lived this way for four years already though, four very turbulent years. It was like being on a small boat. Astray on a wide, stormy ocean.

CHAPTER NINE

Eric was in the back of the café, washing cutlery with a tea towel slung over his shoulder. It was early evening and as I pushed the door open, I heard the radio playing softly. The sound of a tinkling piano resonated within the café, like bells in a temple.

'Davla's been to the funeral today of her mother's friend,' Eric said. 'She called and said she'd be in later. She sounded bad, so I told her to stay home. It's been a manic day too.'

He came over and kissed both my cheeks.

I helped him dry the dishes and eventually we sat down.

'So what's happening babe?' He handed me a beer.

'Well, the job hunting is going well. I'm going to apply for roles in Amsterdam. There's a friend looking out for jobs for me there.'

'It's all going to happen for you, I am so sure.'

'Do you think so?' I asked.

He laughed and took a huge swig of his beer and sat down opposite me, his blue sarong riding up a couple of inches to reveal his skinny ankles.

'Living in Amsterdam will be fun. I've been there a few times and I love it,' he said.

The café seemed subdued, like a meditative place.

Eric had tied his dreads back into a ponytail and his heart shaped face was now clearer. I saw that he had a high forehead and his chin dipped a little sharply. There was an air of gentle flirtatiousness about him.

'Sarah was in earlier, sometimes I think she needs some kind of life compass to get by,' he said.

'What did she say?'

'She was talking about her violent ex-husband and how he ruined her life.'

I was silent.

He looked at me knowingly. 'You and I, we're cut from the same cloth.'

'What do you mean?'

'We understand each other, no explanations needed. How much do you want to know about me?' he asked.

'As much as you want to tell me, I suppose,' I said, feeling flattered by his attention.

'Things at home were really bad in Kenya,' Eric said. 'My parents are strict Christians and my grandfather on my mum's side was an Archbishop. Their strictness became a hindrance to my growth, so I moved out when I was twelve.'

'At *twelve?*'

'Yes, I stayed with different friends. My parents thought I was going mad, they prayed for me all the time.' He laughed loudly. 'Whenever my mother saw me, she would lift her arms up and look at the heavens as if God owed her an answer.'

'So, you started rebelling at twelve?'

'You can call it rebellion if you like. I think maybe it started that way, but it was really a quest for something more. I didn't believe in being forced to go to church and my parents kept telling me that I was bringing shame on them.'

The sun reflected a cosy glow on the café windows as the evening progressed.

'I've been meaning to talk to you for a while,' I said.

'Have you now?' Eric teased and I blushed.

'Let me continue before it gets too awkward,' he said, grinning. 'My Christian background created huge doubts in me about heaven. The idea of going to a *heaven* after I died seemed ridiculous. And there was this one thought that kept coming back to me.'

'What was that?' I asked.

He paused and looked out of the window and in that instant the one thought that had persisted in him was revealed to me like a whisper emerging from within the depths of the café.

If I die, then my happiness is after my death. What's the purpose of joy in this existence if I'm supposed to wait for some kind of utopia?

'That question became the root of my investigations.'

'What question?' I asked, pretending that I'd heard nothing.

'You mean you didn't hear what the café just told you?' he asked me, clasping my hand.

'You can hear it too?' I asked.

'Babe, do you think I'd be wasting my time on this conversation if I couldn't hear it?'

'But nobody else can hear it, that's amazing. I thought I was going mad. What are we picking up in here?' I said.

'It's energy. This is a special place and we're tuned to the vibration in it, it's almost holy. You're searching for a meaning in life and that's given you faith, *seek and you shall find*,' Eric said.

'You mean I'm creating it myself?'

'Actually it is there already, it's just that you want to understand it so much that it's revealing itself to you. It's a spiritual realm you're tapping into because the death of your grandmother has propelled you towards a deeper meaning in life than you were used to. This place is like Dr Who's Tardis, it can transport your mind to other places that exist in the universe because of its unique energy.'

'How can that be?' I asked him and he smiled at me softly.

'I'm sure you know that there are special places around where energy lingers. Davla told me that when she first saw the café, she knew it was the right place. As if it had been blessed before she arrived. She said she felt there was something special about it. It's a shame she wants to leave now,' Eric said.

***

Pieter rolled his eyes, by now he was well on his way to being drunk.

'Nina, seriously, all this talk about energy. What does that mean? I'm worried that your state of mind was vulnerable at that time.'

'Pieter, my state of mind was just fine,' I retorted. 'And if you're going to keep on interrupting me with this negativity, I'll just tell my story to someone else. Someone who gives a damn.'

Pieter became sullen. 'Look, this is not the Nina I know and love. I'm just finding this hard to believe.' His voice was fragile. 'This is a new side to you.'

'No, this is a side you've never noticed, or never dared to believe,' I said. I took his hand to comfort him, but he was cold towards me. It may as well have been a stranger's hand.

'I'm going to continue, Pieter. This is who I am and I thought you'd care enough to see that.'

He nodded slowly and I carried on.

***

I remembered Davla's tarot card, the six of cups. I was on a journey, a very special journey.

Eric lit the candle in the middle of the table and the flame leapt up immediately.

He began to speak of his time in Kenya again.

'Nina, you remind me of how I used to be! When I was sixteen I was really hungry for spiritual growth.' He looked at me expectantly.

'My mind or consciousness did develop further. My search led me to look at many different belief systems and religions. I was on a long quest for the truth, whatever that meant.'

'What beliefs did you look at?' I asked.

'Oh loads, there was raja yoga and that helped me meditate further, African traditional religions, Coptic, Hermetic and Hare Krishna, which centres around traditional Hindi scriptures. I gave them a limit of four days each and usually that was enough to see if it was what

I really wanted. I'd speak to the leaders of the groups too and some became annoyed by my incessant questions.'

'Did this mad search help?' I asked.

'It helped me become wiser but I wasn't really satisfied with their explanations because everything drifted back to this utopia idea *after* death. Unfortunately, there were no kinky sex cults,' he said, laughing. 'I might have stayed more than four days if there had been!'

He finished his beer and opened another bottle.

What is the essence of life as it relates to me? What is it that underlies human existence?

The questions sprang from the café like a fountain coming to life.

'Despite my best efforts, I kept reaching a dead end,' Eric said.

The candle flame flickered furiously from side to side suddenly. We both stared at it at the same time.

'You know what I think when a flame flickers like that? It usually means there's another entity in the room. Perhaps it's your grandmother.'

I wasn't sure if he was being serious or not.

The candle changed colour from a pale yellow to a bright golden colour. The flickering stopped and the shadow of the flame continued travelling along the tops of the mirrors like a subtle intruder.

The café was opening up like a flower that had been asleep too long. The petals were unfolding and the smell of the flowers began rising in the air spreading outwards like a magical perfume, jasmine and rose. The perfume floated around the café.

An incessant chattering filled my ears and it suddenly seemed as if the café was full of people. I felt frightened for a moment and I stepped off my stool.

'Everything's fine,' Eric said. His voice sounded elevated as if he were speaking from somewhere above the café.

Tall shadows lined the walls. They seemed to be coming out of the mirrors and walking into the centre. The shadows were covered in long robes, their arms spun masterfully and they seemed to be speaking a language that I didn't understand. They spoke fast and then slow and in rhythm, like monks chanting in a monastery. The energy from their voices was warm and pulsating. It filled the whole café and the golden light from the candle spread outwards like a mist.

It felt like invisible fingers were lightly touching my skin. Someone was massaging my head and my thoughts slowed down. The chanting filled my head but I still couldn't catch what the monks were saying. It was like a continuous melodic song and it continued at a hectic pace and became faster.

It seemed that all the words merged into one another and became one. The chanting became heavier and the bells louder, until the café was filled with light and chanting and bells all fused into one sound. It was the one sound that I had never heard before in my life.

It was a sound of life and death, hope and despair, of the gnashing of teeth and decay, of being born into a world where nothing is certain and the anxiety of day-to-day living. Paradoxically, it was a sound of beauty and peace, of the eternity that was the reality of the universe, of a place so quiet that time stood still like the surface of a placid lake and of love. Love on such a scale that it made the café expand and pulsate in maddening colours; it made it spin faster and faster. The place became a moment in time, a speck in the vast desert of the universe.

Nan's face appeared in front of me and I felt dizzy and nauseous. She was looking down from the ceiling it seemed, and she had a white scarf on her head. Her gaze held mine for a long time. After a while she vanished like ashes without a trace.

I saw Eric in front of me again.

'Are you ok, honey?' His hand was on my shoulder. He brought me a glass of cold water and a few minutes later my dizziness stopped.

It took a while for the sound in the café to die down and when it did, it left a tinge behind. Something lingered in the air, the faint smell of jasmine and rose.

Eric was watching me. He was sitting sideways on the stool now, his face turned towards me.

'What perfume do you have on?' He looked at me and smiled mysteriously.

I knew that *he knew*.

'Eric, what just happened?' My heart was pounding and I felt lighter than I had in a long time.

'You said you were on a journey. Maybe you just felt the power of it,' he said.

'What was that about, that energy? Who were those monks?'

'This place is an enigma,' Eric said, as if he knew an explanation was needed. 'There's something here that shifts. It moves with our moods and inclinations.'

'Does it mean that I imagined all this? How can we both be doing that?' I asked.

'Nina, who said that we were imagining this? You wanted to know if there was something bigger than death after your nan passed on, what do you think now?' he asked.

'There absolutely must be or I'm losing my bloody mind. I can't believe what just happened!' I was shaking slightly, as if I'd stepped off a terrifying rollercoaster ride and my feet had yet to touch solid ground.

'Good. Now we're getting somewhere. Now finish your beer or I'll assume you want something non-alcoholic,' Eric said, laughing.

***

'Fuck, did this really happen, why didn't you tell me before?' Pieter asked, his face pale. 'Come on, this is too much.'

'Would you have believed me if I'd told you before?'

'No, I'd think you were on something, LSD perhaps.'

'That's why I didn't tell you,' I said.

Pieter looked bewildered.

'I see, it's a crazy woman I'm in love with. I knew there was something different about you from the start, but this, well this, is all like a fantasy, in your head. Were you on medication at the time, anti-depressants perhaps?'

Realising that he'd gone too far, Pieter's tone softened. 'Come on, try and see it from my point of view. You never told me anything like this, now it's overkill. The café changing into a Buddhist temple, that's like something out of Dr Who. No one in their sane mind would believe it.'

'Firstly, I was not on any anti-depressants,' I said, angrily. 'Secondly, it really did happen. It was a feeling of being transported someplace else, outside of this world that we know, another world, another time, another place. And you're right, no one in their sane mind would get that. Perhaps you have to be a little open minded to travel there. Anyway, I'm going to keep going with my crazy tale, if you don't mind.'

***

'Are the others in the café aware of all this?' I asked Eric. 'James would never believe me if I told him.'

'Maybe on some level they do, and that's why James keeps coming back here. I realised it a long time ago. When I saw that no one else noticed, I didn't say anything. I didn't want everyone to think I was nuts.'

'I just saw my nan again and as you know she's already passed away,' I said.

'The Universe mirrors us more than we realise,' Eric said.

'Do you think this place reflects who we really are?' I asked. My heart had stopped pounding and I felt radiant. My mind was focused, as if I'd been cleansed.

'Your thoughts are who you become. You can call it destiny or whatever you like,' Eric said.

'How can your thoughts determine your destiny?'

'Nina, you've already decided to search for something better than the superficial life you were leading and now that you've done that you're moving on to the next level,' Eric said.

'So you think it's because I changed my thinking?' I asked him.

'Yes, absolutely, I do. You're shifting your life, out with the old and in with the new. I'll drink to that!'

'Do you believe in anything out there?' I asked him.

'I'm a Buddhist at heart, sweetie.'

'Are you a serious, practising Buddhist?'

He grinned and pointed his finger at me, his eyes widening.

'I am a Buddhist but *never* a serious one! I don't have a book of do's and don'ts. I just take it a day at a time.'

'And that works?' I asked.

'Faith is different for everyone and you'll have to find your own path and I believe you have already. Hang in there and you'll find what you're looking for.'

His words travelled to a place inside me that I hadn't known existed, where nan's love and memories lay.

The world carries on regardless, I thought. And I felt the sadness in my heart that no one could comfort. Eric was right, there was nothing he or anyone else could do. I was the only one who could reconcile her death with what I believed.

'Put it this way,' Eric said, reaching out to hold my hand. 'You could always join a kinky sex cult until you've figured out what you believe. That way at least you'll have some fun, Amsterdam would be perfect.'

I laughed and we were silent for a while.

Later I walked home in the early hours of the morning with a new elation in my heart. The café had amazed me that evening, it had revealed the greatest show on earth and even beyond. The monks had participated in it and I now knew that the world was far bigger than I'd ever realised. It was a world within a world we lived in.

I wanted to go home and tell James but I knew he wouldn't understand. His rational and intellectual mind wasn't capable of seeing what I'd just witnessed, at least not yet. I thanked God then and I said a prayer for my nan and really wished her well on her journey, wherever she was. I felt the prayer resonate in my heart and I knew I meant it, that somewhere she felt it. I'd been too sad in India at the Ganges to know any better and now I was lifted from that darkness. Death wasn't the end, of that I was certain. It was only the beginning. The evening had been a major turning point for me and I was confident that things would now fall into place. I just had to believe, to re-align my thinking with my desires.

CHAPTER TEN

Soho Square was heaving from every corner when I arrived there just after noon.

A band was setting up near the Greek Street side of the square and the musicians were testing out their equipment. There were a few twangs on the guitar, an occasional roll on the drum and a guy with spiky blond hair setting up the microphone.

***

'So you were just around the corner from here?' Pieter asked me.

'Yes, only two minutes away. Anyway, I was thinking about the café and how I didn't really know anyone there at all. I was feeling down about my general lack of direction in life and wondering what it was all about,' I said.

'Now you're starting to sound like our friend James.' Pieter grinned, sipping another glass of wine. I wondered when he had ordered another bottle and I continued.

***

I sat on the grass as the band started to play. The guy with the spiky hair was a trumpeter, he stood with his eyes closed and started to play. He was in a league of his own. After a while, I noticed Tony. He came over and sat down next to me, just as the trumpeter ended with Miles Davis' track, *So What*.

'Amazing, isn't he?' Tony asked. 'Sarah will be kicking herself for missing this.'

'Where is she?' I asked and he told me that she was talking to Davla in the café.

After the band finished, we headed back to the café.

Sarah, Eric and James were sitting outside at a table, drinking cappuccinos. James was pleased to see me.

'You went off early this morning,' he said.

'How was the music?' Sarah asked.

'It was great, sorry you missed it.'

'Oh, I've seen the trumpeter, Dylan, plenty of times already.'

Tony stood there uncomfortably, waiting for someone to acknowledge him.

Sarah was sitting a little away from the canopy and the sun was almost directly in her eyes, she cupped her hands over them to block it out.

Eric greeted me with a kiss. He was wearing a yellow T-shirt with green palm trees on it, and the words *Paradise Beach* running across the bottom in bright green.

Davla appeared from inside the café, carrying a tray with drinks for a nearby table. She walked past Tony and smiled at him.

The canopy fluttered and the sun disappeared behind a cloud.

'James, you're a bit thoughtful today,' Eric said. 'I haven't heard a peep out of you, what's wrong?'

'I've run out of seminars to go to.' James laughed.

'I rather like him this way,' Davla said.

'Why don't we all grab a late lunch?' Sarah suggested.

'I won't be able to leave the café,' Davla said, a little stiffly.

'Well, the rest of us can go, can't we?'

'How about Japanese?' James said and it was settled.

Sarah said she knew a good restaurant near Leicester Square.

'It's a pity you can't come,' Tony said to Davla.

She didn't answer. Instead she started rounding up empty cups and carried them on the tray back into the café.

James followed Sarah towards Shaftesbury Avenue. Davla watched us from the café for a moment and then she walked to the back.

Eric followed her in. He slipped his arms around her from behind. She seemed to relax against him and whatever he said to her had its tranquil effect. She smiled as she turned to serve a customer.

Saudade. It was a sense of nostalgia that captured the mood in the café for a second, like a feather floating gently in the air.

Give me something familiar for a moment, something I can hold onto and cherish.

Davla's thought at that moment came to me as I stood there, waiting for Eric.

'She feels like she's losing out all the time,' Eric whispered to me. 'That's a shame, how about you? Have you had any luck on the job front yet?'

'It's too early right now, but I am continuing to look abroad.'

'Yes, that might be the way to do it, or have a lover there and stay with him!' Eric suggested playfully.

'Well, there is this Dutch guy….' I started to say.

'Oh, a new man, congratulations!' He gave me a playful punch.

***

'So, you were discussing me with other people already?' Pieter laughed, he sounded pleased.

'I just told them that I'd started seeing you,' I said.

***

Sarah greeted the waitress in Japanese when we arrived.

'That is impressive, where did you learn that?' James asked.

'I travelled to Tokyo with my ex-husband many years ago.'

'A table for five?' the Japanese waitress nodded at Sarah and led us to a round table, big enough for eight people. The restaurant was only half full and smelt like a Chinese herbal shop I'd once visited.

A huge painting of a geisha strolling with a colourful paper umbrella in her hands, her face made up perfectly with white powder and cupid red lips hung on the wall behind us.

I was sitting in-between Sarah and James. Next to James was Tony followed by Eric.

Sarah seemed nervous, as if sitting around a circular table with everyone facing one another put too much emphasis on her. Eric was relaxed. He sipped the sake slowly. Sarah was looking at the palm trees on his T-shirt.

'Where's that? Jamaica?' she asked, nodding in the direction of the T-shirt.

'That is a beach called Paradise Beach. God only knows where it is.' Eric laughed.

'If only there was such a place,' Sarah said, cupping her hands around her green tea. 'Paradise Beach could be where we get the answers to all the difficult questions in life. That would be wonderful, wouldn't it?'

James raised his small glass.

'Cheers to a fine meal,' he said, chuckling. Everyone raised their glasses and said cheers in an enthusiastic tone.

Sarah only raised her glass half way and didn't clink it with anyone else. Her eyes were looking at the green tablecloth, as if she had discovered a great secret woven into it.

Tony sipped his sake quietly, peering over the small glass at everyone as he did so.

The waitress handed Sarah a big bowl of steaming clear broth, floating with all kinds of seafood and vegetables.

'What on earth is that?' Sarah asked, nudging me. 'Nina, can you take a look please?' She pointed at a pale pink piece of flesh floating in the soup.

'I think it's some kind of fish.'

'Why don't you taste it and find out?' Eric said.

'I ordered a seafood dish, and that thing floating around cannot be kosher, just look at it.' She looked like she was about to cry.

'Excuse me, kosher?' James asked.

'*That's right,* kosher! I am Jewish, you know?'

James looked at me with a puzzled expression.

'Can I help you ma'am?' the waitress asked.

'Please can you find out what that is in my soup.' Sarah pointed out the pink flesh.

'That is fish, ma'am,' the waitress replied calmly.

'I would like to know *exactly* what that is,' Sarah said.

'I will find out ma'am.' The waitress bowed slightly in her direction. She was back so quickly that I wondered if she'd really gone anywhere at all.

'It is octopus, ma'am.'

'Octopus!' Sarah turned pale. 'That's not something that I can possibly eat, can't you just get me a vegetarian soup? And another thing, you really don't need to call me ma'am.'

The waitress nodded.

James gave me a bewildered look as if he had no idea what was wrong with Sarah.

'Goodness, how am I going to eat all this?' he said, peering into his packed bento box.

'Sarah, are you okay?' Eric asked quietly.

'Yes, thanks. I just received another letter from my ex-husband and it's kind of ruined my day.'

'Anything you would like to talk to us about?' Eric asked.

'It's just sometimes you know, I wonder if life is meant to be this way. It seems so unfair. I mean he was horrid to me and the kids when they were young and it messed them up for a long time. Now he has the cheek to send me this crap letter telling me he's marrying his long-term girlfriend, Leila. They're going to Brazil on holiday.' She sighed.

'There, there now, don't cry,' Eric said, handing her a tissue.

Tony played with his rice.

The waitress came back with Sarah's soup, leaving it on the table quickly when she saw her crying.

'Excuse me a minute please.' Sarah hurried to the ladies' bathroom.

'Oh dear, she does seem a bit put out,' James said. 'I'm not sure what kind of advice to give in such a dire situation.'

'It's probably best not to say anything,' Tony said.

'Sarah never tells us what's going on, we only see little glimpses,' James said.

'James, you must have seen that she was upset from the word go?' Eric said.

'Yes I did. It's just I don't know how to help her if she never says anything.'

'Maybe she doesn't need your help,' I said.

He looked at me then, his expression momentarily hurt.

'Sometimes we all need help, no man is an island like Eric's t-shirt seems to suggest,' he finally said.

Eric laughed.

'If I knew my shirt was going to get so much attention, I'd have worn another one.'

'It's too happy, that's what I meant,' James said.

'Should I be wearing something more depressing?'

'Not at all. Maybe we can all start calling you agony Uncle Eric. Perhaps you just need to put a phone number on there so we know who to call if we're having a bad day,' James said.

He poured more sake for everyone.

Sarah came back a few minutes later. Her face was washed and she'd applied frosty pink lipstick.

'This soup is much better than the last one,' she said.

Eric looked over at me and I noticed his shapely lips. I remembered the steamy windows in the café and the kiss passing between him and Davla like a soft whisper.

***

'And then I thought of you, Pieter. We were still texting and calling each other then. Our relationship was just beginning and I thought of what it would be like to kiss you,' I said.

'You did?' Pieter smiled, his smile that had enchanted me from the first time I'd met him. The distance between us melted momentarily and we gazed at each other, as if we'd just fallen in love.

'I was missing you at that moment sitting with them all, watching how vulnerable Sarah looked. I wanted to be with you, just forgetting the heavy conversation we were having.'

'That's lovely,' Pieter said, his voice was slurred.

***

Eric was still watching me.

'Angie told me she fancied me initially because I used to look like Paul Newman,' James was saying. 'My wife did have a thing about blue eyes.' He started laughing and Tony joined in.

'Are you okay staying with James?' Sarah asked me, making sure the others weren't listening. 'You know, a young girl like you. You should be careful because you don't know his intentions.'

'He doesn't know mine either,' I said, smiling.

She looked at me for a second as if I were mad. Then she laughed and at the same time, her eyes were searching me thoroughly, trying to read my thoughts. It was clear that she was an inquisitive woman. There was sadness that never left her face though, even as she laughed, as if it were comfortable living amongst the laughter.

'The soup is good,' Sarah told the waitress.

'Thank you, ma'am,' she said, walking away.

'Even I don't call you ma'am!' Tony laughed.

'No, they don't talk like that in East London, do they?' Sarah asked.

'No, thcy don't,' he answered.

They stared at each other like cats in a dark alley. I wondered why there was so much animosity amongst them.

Tony's face had a permanent expression of sadness on it. As if he'd spent his whole life frowning too much and now it was etched there forever.

Sarah looked at me again so that her whole expression was conveyed to me in one instant. And it was the oddest thing, but I felt as if I got a glimpse of something that I wasn't supposed to see, a coded message in her look. It was so brief though, that I wondered if it was my imagination. Her eyes were clear and unhindered; but suddenly they clouded over and became dark like gathering thunderclouds. Helplessness and torment swept over her face like leaves spiralling away caught in a fierce storm. Then it passed.

It was almost as if I was back in the café sitting with her and the café was again revealing to me the depths of her suffering. I wondered if the same energy in the place was carried to the restaurant and how that could be possible. I wanted to ask Eric but he was busy engrossed in conversation with James.

***

'So, you're saying the café woke you up to yourself?' Pieter interrupted me. 'Your tough PR personality was cut through, right? Maybe you recognised something of Sarah's pain in yourself. Your self-awareness must have grown and that's why you could see what was happening with Sarah.'

'Exactly, the café had woken me up to the reality of peoples' lives, something I'd never noticed much before nan died,' I said. 'Now I carried that awareness in me, like a tree that had grown in an unknown territory.'

A person has layers and layers like clothes we all wear.

Nan's voice came to me clearly. She had said that once to my mother in India, when my mother's friend had suffered a nervous breakdown after her marriage collapsed. Nan told my mother that she hadn't seen those problems in her friend properly and she should have done so earlier. I now understood what she meant.

***

'What shall we do later tonight?' James asked us suddenly. 'The night is still young, my dear.'

'I'm heading back to darling Davla,' Eric said patting his stomach.

'Oh, she must be pining for you,' Sarah said and we all laughed.

Outside it was raining lightly, but it was warm.

James decided to leave assuring me that he'd see me later at home. Tony left with him.

'Hey, where's Sarah?' Eric asked me.

'I've no idea. She was here a second ago.'

'She's gone the crazy woman.' Eric laughed. 'She slipped away right under our nose. Come on let's go and keep that Brazilian babe happy for a while.'

He started to walk towards Soho and I followed him wondering where Sarah was. I saw her at the corner of the street. She was a good hundred metres away, jostling her way through a group of people.

'Sarah!' I shouted and Eric stopped ahead of me and turned around.

She stopped and looked back. I couldn't see her face clearly, I thought she would turn back and come towards us and we could all go to the café together.

She didn't come back. She wanted to be alone now, her concern was not with us and her indifference bothered me. I returned to walk beside Eric.

'Is she having one of her turns?' he asked, pulling a face. 'Ah well, leave her to it,' he said cheerfully, weaving his arm through mine as we walked.

The rain became harder and we walked faster, running across Shaftesbury Avenue.

The familiar canopy came into view. I could spot it now from a distance because I knew what I was looking for. The Brazilian flag was emblazoned in the corner like a lucky motto.

The café door was closed tight and the interior looked dim through the glass window as Eric pushed the door open. Davla was sitting alone on the back table reading a book and drinking a glass of red wine. A half empty bottle stood on the table.

'We're back,' Eric said loudly.

'Where are the rest?' she looked up, her expression sour.

I stepped in behind him and the café embraced me with Davla's mood. It was rotten but I didn't care. My own mood was scarcely better than hers because I was thinking about Sarah. Sarah with her sad eyes that told a million tales.

***

'Why were you bothered about her? I mean you hardly knew her. She sounds like a crazy old witch anyway.' Pieter laughed.

'It's just that look she gave me in the café. It was like I saw her suffering then and it really bothered me,' I said.

'Nina, you can't change that, what could you have done? There are plenty of people suffering in this world, you can't help them all, surely you know that by now?' My practical Dutch husband was back, logic firmly screwed on.

'I *know* that!' I hissed. 'But the reason it hit me was because it reminded me of how my mother used to look at me every time my father was cruel to her. You know how I told you it started when I was in my teens. He started to erupt into fits of anger. He'd accuse my mother of stupid things like not cleaning the bath properly and he'd strike her one across the face. She'd creep away into her room like a mouse. It was the same look of dread and helplessness that came over my mother's face that I saw in Sarah's face and it made me hate my father all over again.'

'How did he change?' Pieter asked. 'Honestly, I wish you'd told me about his violence before. I will never speak to that bastard anymore, why didn't you tell me? I feel like you don't trust me, my own wife does not trust me.'

'It's not that Pieter, he was never a really loving father,' I said. 'He'd call my mother spineless and ignore her when she spoke to him. Have you ever seen someone's confidence crumbling away like that? That's what happened and it's horrible.

'As it turned out he *was* having an affair with a woman who was an old friend of his from Paris. And after the French bitch dumped him a year later, my mother still took him back. Can you believe it? She told me she felt sorry for him.'

'An affair? Oh shit, this gets worse. It's probably best not to remember those times,' Pieter said.

'Seeing Sarah like that brought those memories back and when I returned to the café with Eric I felt pretty bad,' I explained. 'I started doubting myself and why I was there, these lessons that I was learning, did they have a purpose?

'Why was this understanding of people's lives becoming apparent to me, did I need that knowledge? And at that moment I wanted to be away from there, I wanted to be with my friends talking about superficial things, I needed to escape.

'I mean these people meant nothing to me and they had no real place in my life. And I had no place in theirs either. Who cared if Sarah was having a crap day? People did all the time and we accepted that was life. I felt an impatience sweep over me that I had never noticed before. Damn that café, there was something about it that was affecting me now, something that was starting to invade my consciousness. It was like an invisible vapour that I was breathing in every day.'

'Why didn't you just walk out and escape?' Pieter asked. 'It all sounds like a bad dream and perhaps it was. Maybe you were just trapped in a nightmare in your head that you couldn't get out of. It's called suffering, Nina, and we all get that during our lives. The stress of it all must have overwhelmed you.'

'It did not overwhelm me,' I snapped. 'You are though, with your negativity! It wasn't a dream and I didn't imagine it. Perhaps you're so stuck where you are, that your imagination has stopped working.'

Pieter looked at me, shocked. The wine had numbed him into silence for now, so I continued.

'I should have taken that step back onto the street and left that bloody moment where it was, suspended in time like a speck of dust,' I said. 'I should have left then and there and never looked back. But I couldn't do it Pieter, I felt compelled to stay. I could have taken a different turn on my journey and I would never have seen Davla or any of them again. I could have moved out of James' flat, I would be gone and who in the world would care?'

'But you didn't do it Nina and there's the mystery, why not? If that were me, I'd have run away and kept going and never looked back,' Pieter said, quietly.

'It was a message that I couldn't ignore any more, about people and their struggles. I was facing a dilemma, I felt like the Buddha living in my palace in my luxurious life and suddenly I was out of it in the real world. How can you ignore that?' I asked.

'Plenty of people do, but now you're comparing yourself to the Buddha! For God's sake Nina, you're not the Buddha,' Pieter said.

'I know I'm not the fucking Buddha,' I said, exasperated and the couple next to our table looked at me strangely. I took a deep breath and calmed down. 'Can you let me finish in peace?' I asked Pieter and he nodded.

'I realised that I still needed answers and that they were rooted in that café,' I said.

***

'So I stood there like a dope as Eric hugged Davla, her desolate mood hanging like cobwebs from every corner of the café and I felt so lonely and isolated that a sharp physical pain *actually* went through me and I winced. I felt as if I were watching the drama unfold in that place, I was taking in every breath of someone else's sadness and now it was showing me my own pain. At that time, I thought again damn this café, this stupid café, it's starting to make me face my own issues, it's really starting to drive me mad.'

CHAPTER ELEVEN

In hardly any time at all Eric had grabbed a stool for me at Davla's table, poured me some wine and told me to sit down. He patted the seat of the stool twice to encourage me, but it still looked uninviting.

'Was the food in the restaurant your idea of heaven?' Davla asked Eric.

'It was good but Davla, you know I don't believe in heaven,' Eric said, smiling.

'Oh yeah, you're a Buddhist, aren't you? They don't believe in God do they?'

She looked over at me as if I could somehow answer that question. Her face looked drained.

'Nina did you have a good time? You're a bit quiet today.'

'She's cool. Leave her alone. God knows, I'm sure you've eaten Japanese food before, haven't you Davla?' Eric said, mildly irritated.

'Of course I have, anyway, I thought you didn't believe in God?' Davla said sharply.

'You got me there.' Eric started laughing.

'I'm sorry. I'm feeling rubbish today. The funeral made me very sad,' Davla said.

'Oh babe, come here,' Eric said, gently.

Davla leant forwards and edged her stool closer to Eric. He put his arm around her. I finally sat down.

'You didn't miss much, honestly. I had a debate with James about religion. As we all know, he's obsessed with God, then he started saying he looked like Paul Newman when he was younger. Doesn't he go on about it when you're at home with him Nina?' Eric asked.

It took me a moment to realise that he had directed his question at me. It was only when I saw that they were both staring at me that I nodded hastily, and Eric laughed.

'I can see that we're all a little tired tonight,' he commented.

'James' favourite topic, as everyone knows, is his wife,' I said.

The café seemed to accommodate us perfectly now as they listened to me. The hostile mood that had greeted me was dissipating fast and it was becoming peaceful. I felt myself relax.

'Sarah was in a funny mood,' Eric said. His eyes were fixed on the candle flame, as if he were being hypnotised by it.

'Oh, that's nothing new. I think maybe she's got something wrong with her, up there?' Davla pointed her finger on her left temple.

'That's not very nice,' Eric said, scolding her gently.

'I think the woman is strange, okay?' Davla jumped up, startling us both. Eric's arm hung in mid-air for a second as if he didn't know what to do with it. He slowly brought it back to his side and gave me a weary look.

She's really trying me today.

Davla sat down again and we were silent for a while.

'I do wonder sometimes why I'm here at this point in time,' Davla said.

'Where?' Eric asked.

'Here, in this café.'

'I thought you meant here, as *in this world*, not this little café. Just chalk it up to experience.'

'That's what my mother always says. I mean, are we supposed to spend half our lives just fucking experiencing things? What about doing what we *really* want to do?' Davla said loudly.

'You are doing what you originally wanted to do,' Eric reminded her.

Davla swore in Portuguese under her breath, and although we didn't understand her, her words sounded bitter to me.

I looked at Eric and the absurdity of the situation struck me. Here I was listening to someone else's tales of woes. It was enough.

I stood up and the café appeared to grow darker around me.

Eric looked at me curiously.

'Are you off then?' he asked, his voice hinting urgently that I should stay.

I started to say that I had things to do, that James was expecting me home.

I imagined that James would now be reading up on theories about God and his existence, or novels by Tolstoy and Dostoevsky. His loneliness would be wrapped around him, as close as the favourite navy robe that he wore. James, who was denying that living without his wife was probably driving him slowly mad.

I laughed out loud at my thoughts and Eric asked me what was so funny.

'This whole situation is funny.'

He egged me on with a gentle nod.

'Here I am, and I don't even really know you guys. I don't even know what I'm doing here. I feel like I took a wrong turning somewhere.'

They both remained quiet.

'Oh, *bollocks* to that, is that the right word to say? I was thinking all that rubbish earlier,' Davla finally said. 'There's no point in thinking like that. It leads nowhere. When I was at home, if things got too heavy, you know what we would do? We'd throw great parties. With lots of beer and music and tasty men, mostly that did the trick, well for a while anyway. And in the morning, I'd wake up and the sun still shone and everything was OK. When I was a young girl, my father was my rock and I was his doting daughter. Then I grew up and things changed and became sad and difficult really. I understood that nothing stays the same forever.' She finished.

I'm not alone in this craziness.

Her words reached me loudly and it seemed that Eric heard them too as he suddenly looked around as if he sensed something in the air.

'There's more wine in the back,' Davla said to Eric and he was already gone, looking for it.

I sat down again and the walls behind Davla flickered with the shadow of an orange glow until it seemed as if the whole café was becoming engulfed in soft orange dust that floated in the air.

Eric opened another bottle of white wine and poured everyone a glass.

Nobody else came into the café that evening. It was as if people knew that they should stay away. A few did look in and some even hesitated and searched the front windows for a clue as to what lay inside. They discovered none and so never came in.

The wine was making me tipsy. At one point, Eric looked at his watch and told Davla that he had promised to see another friend that evening.

'Nina will keep you company, come on babe, this is my colleague David's goodbye do, he's going to America. I said I'd stop by.'

He kissed her quickly and stood up.

'Laters.' He pushed hard on the door, waving at me.

The door closed back upon itself slowly and Davla and I were alone.

After Eric's departure, I thought about making my excuses and leaving, but just at that moment and as if she were reading my thoughts, Davla asked me if I was drunk.

'I'm getting there definitely.'

'Me too, you're staying a while, aren't you?'

'I… yes, I will stay for a bit.'

Afraid to live, that's what I am, afraid to really live.

Her thought glided by me like a passing bird.

She silently looked outside the window and took a large sip of her wine.

I was wondering if I should grab a book off the shelf and start to read it. I needed to do something, *anything*.

'Listen,' she said suddenly, in an impatient manner. 'I'm going to sell this fucking café once and for all and move on, what do you think about that, Nina, huh?'

'Davla, that's really up to you.'

She gave me a stare that suggested I was being unhelpful. It was a warrior's stare, intense and heated, ready to do battle.

***

'It sounds like if looks could kill you'd have been dead,' Pieter said. 'The ice princess from Brazil, that's a contradiction in itself.'

'She wasn't that bad,' I said.

'So now you're defending her?' Pieter said. 'How am I supposed to take this?'

'Take it any way you want. I'm telling you how it was and Davla was cool. Are you drunk, Pieter?' I asked him.

'Nina, we've been sitting here for ages drinking wine and whisky. I'm going with the flow.'

'Well, that evening Davla was going with her flow too, she was also really drunk,' I said.

***

Davla finished the wine and she opened the fridge and took out another bottle. She was so drunk that she swayed for a moment.

Her feet wobbled in her heels. She started giggling and
soon we were both laughing.

'Jesus, look at me, what a mess I am. Who would have
thought it would come to this?' she giggled.

The wine gave her the courage to speak about matters of the heart. She was able to express her thoughts better. Eventually they escaped through her voice.

The café brought her thoughts to the surface and they floated there like a vapour.

She's been the constant thorn in my side, she makes me feel like I am worth nothing.

'It's you and me again,' Davla said and her voice was slightly slurred. 'We've got to stop meeting like this, honey. People might start talking.' She started laughing again and I joined in. She grabbed my arm and a shadow crossed her face.

'Nina, you know you told me about your grandmother and how lovely she was, well, I have a confession to make. That made me really jealous because I wish I'd had that closeness with my mother. I always wanted her to acknowledge me and she pushed me away so much that I stopped expecting anything. In London, things got so bad with my mother that I had to leave home.'

She let go of my arm and I could still feel the heat from her hand there burning.

Ribbons of red emanated from the café. They played across Davla's face tantalisingly but she barely noticed.

The heat in the café became intense. I opened the door and the cool air helped me to break away from the spell in the café.

Davla's energy was restless. The red ribbons danced above her head, they circled the lights above me and bounced off the counter. They were her thoughts and they became clearer to me.

I hate the way mum treats me, why can't she tell me that she loves me? Life's too fucking short to waste, I keep telling her that. But it's like she's closed herself off from me.

'Why does your mother treat you that way, Davla?'

'That's the million dollar question. Who the fuck knows? Maybe God does.'

She finished her wine in one gulp and sighed.

'I feel like I've become a warrior – you know inflexible and rigid. I'm always on my guard, always observing. I know my actions can be like a sledgehammer and I sometimes cut people off. It's from years of protecting myself from her coldness, Jesus, I'm used to this battle now.'

'I've seen glimpses of your anger and impatience, usually with James,' I said.

'Sometimes James scares off other customers with his silly debates,' she said.

'My mother is weak and always lets my father put her in her place. When I watch her reacting to him calling her a slut or a useless cow, I just want to beat her myself,' I said.

Davla shook her head and frowned.

'That's so scary. My mother believes in herself so much that she's become a goddess, a super controlling powerful bitch. We're so different. Yes, I'm a warrior but even warriors need to rest and regain their strength. The truth is that I'm tired of being strong. Years of being strong are starting to break my back, do you know what I should do?' Davla pleaded.

I shook my head.

'Thank God for Eric,' Davla continued. 'He's a good friend and he makes me laugh and that breaks the terror that sometimes burns in me. Nina, you seem so wise, was it your grandmother who made you that way? What is your secret?'

'I don't have a secret,' I said. 'Talk to Eric, he's good for you.'

'Isn't he great? I like him a lot. I think he fancies you,' Davla said, looking at me closely, her voice slightly slurred.

I blushed and started denying it.

'Oh come on darling, you must have noticed.' Davla waved her hand, dismissing my denials.

'Does it bother you?' I asked.

'Not in the least, he has a soft spot for you.' She winked at me.

I finished my drink quickly.

'Eric is a Piscean, he's emotional and deep and he calms me down, his water puts out my fire. He doesn't give up on me either, even when I give up on myself.'

Davla was sitting close to the candle and the flame was burning low.

'Sometimes I hear my mother's critical voice like a thunderclap and it makes me lose my confidence,' Davla said.

'Did you ever talk about it with your dad?' I asked.

'All the time. He only responded with a sad smile, as if there were family skeletons in the closet that he wasn't willing to let out. After approaching him a few times, I gave up. Afterwards, my loneliness pierced me like a spear but no one could feel it except me. So many times I came back home to a screaming mother and a father who tried to keep the peace, always failing in his mission.

'You know my mother told me on my sixteenth birthday that I was her first born child and she loved me unconditionally. In her next sentence she told me that I was too wayward and I reminded her of someone she used to know.'

'So she gave you love with one hand and took it all away with the other?' I said.

'Exactly. What a mother! Full of surprises. She ruined my birthday and she never told me who I reminded her of. Maybe a dopey whore she saw somewhere in town.'

'Davla, don't be ridiculous.'

She laughed.

'I'm only joking.'

I was surprised at the tears that pricked her eyes.

Suddenly the café threw the answer at me. Everything became transparent, like a vivid dream. I knew what had happened to her.

Who was that person Davla's mother had been talking about? It could only have been herself.

***

'How did you know that, was it intuition or are you becoming a clairvoyant now?' Pieter asked.

'It was strong intuition and the café gave me that answer, I swear.'

'How is that logically possible?' Pieter asked.

'It's not, I realise that but that café housed a lot of secrets and I think I was meant to understand them to see how complex we humans are.'

'Hmmm, that's just another theory of yours. Can I call it that?' Pieter asked. 'This whole story is riddled with mysteries that I can't fathom.'

'You can call it what you want, but it's the truth,' I said.

'Your truth perhaps, darling,' Pieter said and I felt a distance divide us. Something told me that if I continued, this could be bad for my marriage, yet I felt compelled to carry on.

***

'Perhaps your mother was talking about herself?' I said to Davla and she nodded.

'I think so. I often wonder if there was a secret in my family that I didn't know about. Why else would she treat me that way?' Davla asked.

'Do you want to know what I think?'

'Tell me, Nina. Other people see these situations clearer.'

And the café spoke to me gently and it was my nan's voice that I heard. She whispered in my ear softly. I remembered standing at the great Ganges River and my heart was bleeding that day and the heat was overwhelming me. Now her voice was whispering in my ear and I knew what I had to say to Davla.

'Your mother loves you very much,' I said, gently. 'When she looks at you, she remembers the dreams that she was not allowed to follow herself because of her own strict parents. Your mother sees a beautiful young woman, who looked like she must have when she was younger, but who in comparison is as free as the ocean. You ran away and followed your heart, the one thing that she was never allowed to do,' I said.

Davla was crying quietly, wiping her tears away roughly with the back of her hand. 'My mother told me that she was denied a lot, she told me that my grandparents were very strict,' Davla said. 'It's almost like she takes out on me what was denied to her. My grandmother told me that she had an arranged marriage as she wasn't allowed to date anyone without their permission. But there's more to her story, I'm sure of it.'

***

'How can you be sure about everything you told her?' Pieter asked.

'Because Davla said it was true herself,' I replied.

I turned to Pieter. 'It was at that moment that I understood the truth of it and Davla did too. It was as if a thick curtain was finally pushed aside to reveal what was behind it.'

'What was the truth?' Pieter asked, his voice sombre.

***

'Do you think it's possible that my dad isn't my real dad?' Davla asked me.

'Why do you say that?' I asked.

'Once I overheard my parents talking when I was twelve. I heard my mother tell my dad that he shouldn't tell me about it. I rushed into the kitchen and asked him what they were talking about. They were really surprised to see me so I knew it was major, whatever it was.'

'What happened then?' I asked.

'I tried to joke about it but it was awkward. I asked dad if he was my real father and my mother slapped me. I rushed out of the room but not before I saw the look on my dad's face. It was a look of pain I'd never seen before and I felt terrible, as if I'd discovered a shameful secret. We never spoke about it again but that look still haunts me.'

'Your mother might have lost the man she loved because her parents forced her to stop seeing him. He may have been your real father. Maybe your grandparents arranged for your mother to marry someone else, your father now.'

Davla was shivering. I made her a cup of tea and she drank it, but she was still trembling.

'Your words have a ring of truth around them and that scares me. That would mean that my mother was already pregnant when she got married and that the father I know, isn't my real one. By the time he knew she was pregnant with another man's child, it was too late. Oh Jesus, I can't stop shaking,' Davla said.

I put my arm around her, she smelt faintly of jasmine perfume.

'They must have tried to make their marriage work for my sake. I'm sure my father loves my mother and that's what's blinded him to his duty, even if he was furious about it. We moved a lot when I was little, from neighbourhood to neighbourhood as if we were escaping. Mother could never forget the love of her life and every time she sees me, she must see him. Oh God, she's forced to see him every day.'

Davla dabbed her eyes roughly with a napkin, wiping her streaking mascara off her face.

'I think every time my mother looks at me she remembers the silent discarding of her dreams. The life that she wanted was closed forever, like a dusty old book. I must be a paradox to her, I am the love and the heartbreak of her life and she can't reconcile the two,' she said.

***

'Wow, is that the truth?' Pieter asked. 'That's kind of heavy. Did you and Davla believe in your theory?'

'Yes and it wasn't a theory, it was intuition and guidance. I felt bad as I couldn't offer Davla any real comfort, it must have been a shock for her. The café wasn't hiding anything from us that evening,' I said.

'No, it certainly wasn't,' Pieter said. 'Intuition and guidance – it's all alien to me.'

'Davla said that her mother stopped telling her she loved her,' I said. 'So she turned to other men instead and sometimes a resemblance of that deep love did come through from one or another, but it always faded in time. It was as if the café flung the face of Davla's mother into its midst that evening.'

'That's spooky, I think we need a break from all this for a while,' Pieter said. 'Your story is very supernatural, you've never explained it in so much detail and now it's overwhelming me. It's like I'm seeing a new side to you and frankly, it is a little scary. I need to get to know you all over again. I'm a banker, not a magician!'

'Too much of a banker,' I muttered.

'What did you say?' he asked, his voice was vulnerable.

'Nothing, just that I can imagine it is a lot to get your head around. So I'll just finish this part for now.'

***

'It's time to close up,' Davla whispered hoarsely, she looked around the café. The books lay on the shelves eerily, like silent witnesses to the events of the evening.

Davla looked like she was still trying to shake off the image of her mother, so strong in the café, like an unwanted and troublesome customer. She bade me goodnight and kissed me on both cheeks. Her breath was hot and she pressed her warm hand into mine.

'Shall I walk you to the bus stop?' I asked.

'I'll get a cab,' she replied firmly.

She dialled the number for the cab office and before she got through she thanked me for being there that evening. She sat on her stool restlessly, with her mobile in her hand. The window reflected her image back and it was hazy and distorted.

'I guess everything has a reason and today we've figured that out. We know something's wrong Nina, but my parents will never admit it and that's what I'm so sad about.'

CHAPTER TWELVE

'I feel like I'm rediscovering you all over again,' Pieter said. 'Yet all this Nina, this café and James and Davla, picking up on their thoughts and knowing that Davla's dad was really another man. Well, you'll excuse me for being sceptical, won't you?'

'Pieter, you know I wouldn't lie to you. It's like I'm losing you the more I tell you what happened. Your disbelief is making me sad.'

'I know, I do *know* that. It just seems so incredible though. I just want to know if that all really happened. You know the chanting you heard in the café that night you were with Eric, is it possible that you imagined it? Perhaps you missed your grandmother so much that you just wanted to find a place where you felt safe?' Pieter suggested, for the umpteenth time. 'Your safety was gone. Maybe you were temporarily.'

'What, insane? Just say it because that's what you're thinking!'

'No, I don't mean that.' He looked desperate and I had an urge to kiss him, but I held back.

'I was searching for answers but I'm not deluded enough to make up this story,' I said.

'I'm not saying you made it up, you were obviously looking for something after she died, maybe you were so anxious to find an answer that you, I don't know…' he shrugged.

'Pieter, I feel like you don't trust me or believe my story.'

'I'm sorry.' Pieter grabbed my hand. 'Maybe Dutch people are just too logical.'

We sat quietly and I felt disheartened as Pieter held my hand. It was already five in the afternoon now and the crowds were disappearing. Pieter watched groups of people walk past absently.

'You know that I was brought up in a Christian household and the days of going to church with my family are so long gone that I can't even call myself a nominal Christian,' Pieter said, letting go of my hand and turning to face me.

'Nina, I know you wouldn't lie, but there is a part of me that's fighting what you're telling me because it challenges the faith I was brought up with. If what you're saying is true, it means that reality is a lot bigger than I ever imagined. It means man's nature is different to what I thought existed and we don't turn to dust when we die but go on spiritually to another life. That means there's a whole new world out there that's exciting and full of possibilities, but who would believe me if I told them?' He stopped and nodded in the direction of the café.

'If those events really took place in this shabby looking café, what am I to make of that?' he asked.

'Those events did happen. Somehow the café did turn into a temple that evening with Eric, and I could read peoples' thoughts too. If that sounds crazy, then so be it. There are some things that science just can't explain. If you keep worrying about what people think you'll never explore anything, and forever be a slave to the systems that be,' I said.

'God, we are getting too serious about this,' I added, but he remained silent. 'We're meeting the others later tonight, don't you remember? I said we'd be in Old Compton Street at eight.'

'What I don't get is why Eric didn't tell you that the café was closed when he emailed you,' Pieter said.

'It might have still been open then or maybe he knew it would upset me,' I replied.

***

I had come into work about a month earlier and found an unexpected email from Eric. It was the first one since I'd left London. I had never known his surname, but it was Adoyo, Eric Adoyo. I remember giving him my email address years ago, for an account that I hardly looked at. For some reason that day I decided to check. When I realised it was him, I couldn't quite believe it. His message read:

Dear Nina,

I hope my email reaches you safely. I've been thinking a lot about you lately and wondering how you are. Your silence is deafening, you haven't contacted any of us since you left and I miss you. There must be a good man in your life keeping you busy! Did it work out with that guy in Amsterdam? Babe, so much has happened since you left. Sadly, my dad died in Kenya six months after you'd gone and so I gave up my job and went home for a year because my mum was very depressed and struggling to cope. I had to find another job when I came back and so I ended up temping in random offices all over London. Unlike you, I never did pick up my father's energy in the café, so I found it lonely and hard. There was no one I could talk to. Nina, I've been searching for you for a long time. I long for our chats and that level of understanding we had. I hope this is your email address, because if it's not, I might just give up trying to find you.

If you get this, can you meet me the next time you're in London? There's a lot I have to tell you, but face to face. Your friend, Eric

It seemed to me that he had written the email cautiously as if he'd contemplated every word. I replied back immediately explaining that I was coming to London shortly and gave him my contact number. The next morning he called me at work.

'Nina babe, is that really you?' His voice sounded subdued, as if he didn't dare believe it was me.

'Yes, it's great to hear from you again.'

'I wondered if we'd speak again in this lifetime.' And he laughed the same hearty laugh he'd always had. 'I forgot the name of your company, darling, I'm so sorry. I've contacted all the PR companies in Amsterdam looking for you, it's been mad. I kept asking for Nina, I don't know your surname and I only had your old email address, don't you ever check it?'

I apologised to him and I was about to ask how the others were when I had to deal with an urgent work matter. I tried to call later but his phone was engaged. I was extremely busy, so I only emailed Eric two days before I came to London, promising to meet him at the café. His short email back said that Davla wanted to catch up with me too. I was suddenly excited because it felt like old times again.

I hadn't been back to Soho for five years and the prospect of going back with a husband to meet everyone was thrilling. I forgot about work and decided to enjoy myself in London. Little did I realise the café was closed.

***

'It is odd Eric didn't say anything,' Pieter said, looking at the older couple walking past the café.

'Do you remember when we went to Morocco for our honeymoon and we got stuck in the desert and those Bedouins had to rescue us and push our car out of the sand? Shit, there must have been ten of them. They scared the hell out of me but the thought of dying in the desert was even worse. It seems like a long, long time ago already.' Pieter paused and fiddled with his empty glass, before pouring himself more wine.

'Do you believe me about the café then?' I asked.

Pieter sighed and sat back in his chair.

'There's a part of me that does and there's another part that resists. Put it this way, if someone else had told me they'd been to the café and had all those supernatural adventures, I'd think they were mediums or wonder if they were on drugs. But because it's you, I wonder if it's possible, that God directed you to that place. Yet, I'm still fighting it. It's like a new Nina is emerging from this place, the café, and she's not my safe, predictable wife anymore,' Pieter said.

I felt like a punch had hit me in the stomach.

'Safe, predictable? Thanks Pieter. I didn't realise that you thought of me so fondly.'

'I do, I do,' Pieter said, hastily. Much to my dismay, he laughed. 'I suppose it could be true that your grandma was with you in the café. She obviously loved you to bits so perhaps that café is blessed in some way and that's why it's special, but I can't swallow that.'

'I have to admit, it bothers me that you don't believe me,' I said.

'I know, but I can't pretend. I'm rational, life is life, death is death. All this airy fairy business about life after death. No one really knows do they? It's all faith at best and a guess, at worst,' Pieter said.

Since we had never discussed the café in such detail before, I realised that we hadn't explored our beliefs and faiths. Even after his mother had died, Pieter had been so busy dealing with his work and family that he had only attended church to pray for her twice.

I loved Pieter because of the richness of his spirit, his search for adventure and his humour. We had laughed a lot when I had first arrived in Amsterdam and we had started dating. He hired a male stripper dressed as a Dutch policeman on my birthday and he had coaxed me into sharing a massive joint with him later. Yet he was serious about his work too and he knew how to balance his personality with mine.

It mattered to me greatly that his family were kind to me and his twelve-year-old brother, Wouter, immediately liked me.

Pieter's father was a well paid consultant who worked in banking security and his mother had been a music teacher. They lived in a huge house near Vondel Park, a wealthy part of Amsterdam. I found his father more approachable in the beginning. After a year, his mother had warmed to me more and she started inviting us both over for dinner once a week. She played the piano beautifully and taught a few students. Once she played Chopin to the whole family and it moved me to tears. I was reminded of James and how he had once said that 'Words are like a melody, like Chopin would have played as his fingers flowed like water over the piano.'

I vowed to send James a letter then. I wrote it and was about to send it the next day when the unimaginable happened. Pieter's mother had a heart attack unexpectedly alone at home one morning. His father found her slumped over the piano during the afternoon. That was in my third year in Amsterdam and I completely forgot to send James the letter. In the end, I must have thrown it away by mistake.

At the funeral, Pieter cried openly and left a poem he had written to his mother by her grave. We had been talking about getting married but we left it for another six months. Pieter spent more time with his family and I felt he was detached from me for a while. I gave him his space and focused on building my career instead. I worked hard and socialised more with work colleagues.

After those six months, Pieter and I were having dinner in a Tibetan restaurant, when he suddenly opened a small box with a simple gold ring in it and asked me to marry him. We didn't sleep that night. I later asked him if he was really ready for marriage, and he said he was.

I was totally over the moon and we announced it to both our families the following day. His father was delighted and insisted on paying the deposit on a new house for us to buy together. We didn't have a big crowd on our wedding day as we'd only invited immediate family and a close circle of friends. The next day we flew to Morocco for our honeymoon.

I poured more wine and took a sip, just as Pieter's voice cut into my thoughts.

'What are you thinking about? You're a world away, it's not about James again, I hope. I'm done with his love for you.'

'Pieter, just stop this nonsense,' I said.

'Isn't it funny, your story seems to be creating a divide between us. Should we stop now or leave it until it's too late?'

'If our marriage is strong enough, this shouldn't cause a divide,' I said.

Pieter's eyes welled up but he hastily brushed the tears away.

'If you don't accept me for who I am,' he began.

'Excuse me, who isn't accepting who here? It's certainly not me. I came here to tell you about the café and you've been scoffing at me all afternoon. Maybe you're just a traditional, boring guy after all.'

Now I had the tears in my eyes. Pieter ignored me, so the distance between us started to become a gulf.

We both looked at a laughing couple standing opposite outside the café. The man hugged the woman and lifted her off her feet as she shouted and one of her shoes dropped off. He picked it up and put it back on her foot.

'I think they're completely pissed,' Pieter said. 'And it's coming up to half six now, do you think Eric will show up?'

'Eric will come,' I said, sounding despondent.

The couple moved on and the café looked dark and misplaced in a busy street with a bustling patisserie next to it.

'I wonder what will happen to the café,' Pieter said, turning to look at me. 'What happened next after you saw Davla that night? We don't have much time, so can you tell me the rest. Somehow, I think you're going to anyway.'

CHAPTER THIRTEEN

I knew James was gone even before I got out of bed. There was none of the usual knocking on my door or frantic urgency of his voice telling me that tea was ready *now*. The flat felt despondent.

There were signs that he had left earlier during the morning and I was sorry that I had missed him. His cup of tea on the kitchen table was cold and he had already washed his breakfast plates. I went to shower and noticed that it was already ten thirty.

The door to his room was firmly closed and it made the hallway seem darker, so I opened it.

Even with the window open, it was hot in his room. He had been reading a biography about Marcel Proust. Something about the room was *different*. I swivelled around quickly and in that single action, I saw what it was.

He had stacked up photographs of Angela around the candle. I flicked through them hastily.

I wanted to understand what it was that James was going through. There must be millions of people like him in the world, I reasoned with myself, who went through similar painful emotions every day. I thought that if I understood him, I would understand myself better too. I was a silly idealist perhaps or a fool.

I sat down on the sofa and went through his photos again slowly. The sofa coaxed me gently and I felt myself sink deeper into it.

***

'So you were having a good nose around?' Pieter asked. 'What were you hoping to find? Were you interested in him, Nina? Just tell me, I promise I won't make fun of you.'

'Not at all, it was just the perfect opportunity! The emptiness that I'd felt earlier in the summer about nan was being replaced by a gradual remembrance of her ways and mannerisms, the very things that make us unique,' I said.

'Nan told me once that if she could put all her treasured memories in a jar she would carry it around with her. In it she would have snippets of conversation, smiles; words said between families that glued them together, anything that made us who we were. Once she told me that she had forgotten that I was only ten.'

'So her memory spurred you on?' Pieter asked.

'Yes because I was changing and now I was determined to look for work again, I was ready,' I said.

***

Davla was busy talking to Sarah near the counter, she saw me come in and said hello and then carried on with her conversation. They both spoke in urgent hushed tones, their voices carried into the very corners of the café.

I spent the next few hours making phone calls and speaking to old and new media contacts. Later I went to an internet café nearby and applied online for two jobs in Amsterdam that you Pieter, had suggested. Afterwards, I headed back to the café.

Sarah was sitting alone writing and Davla was reading a magazine behind the counter, her hair tied up in a tight ponytail.

Sarah wrote deftly, so that I could hear the noise the pen made as she hurriedly rushed it across the page. It was as if she had to get her frustration out on the paper. She hadn't even greeted me yet and I didn't know if she'd seen me or not. I was out of breath when I arrived at the café, my mind still fresh with the words of my covering letters.

All three of us were so absorbed that we didn't notice James come in moments after me. He entered as if he was a shadow and the café reflected that shadow upon its wall. He said hello quietly to Davla and she looked up from her magazine.

James had a bulging satchel slung over his shoulder. It could easily have belonged to one of his former students. He bumped into a stool as he made his way over to me and Sarah looked up, her pen poised in the air.

'Hello Sarah.' He acknowledged her with a quick nod.

She smiled and carried on writing, almost afraid that she would miss something important.

James sat down next to me. It seemed his mood was cast over and he noticed that I was out of breath.

'My dear, you just beat me here, you are always rushing.' His words stopped me in my tracks. They were spoken with such tenderness that they reminded me of how nan used to speak to me.

Nina, you're like a high-speed train, rushing around from one station to the next, never stopping for breath, slow down child.

I saw loneliness etched on his face like a tattoo.

'How is the job hunting coming along?' he asked.

'I've filled in a couple of applications already today.'

'Glad to hear it. I must say, you'll be missed when you go. You won't forget us when you're stepping up the career ladder will you?'

'James, I've only just started applying for jobs, give me a chance.' I laughed but he didn't join in.

'I hope you remember me and this small flat in Covent Garden.' His voice sounded heavy suddenly.

'You're getting sentimental now. Do you think I'd go away and not remember this summer at all?'

He was listening to me intently, as if he'd wanted me to say that a long time ago.

'I'm not the sort of person who cared to look at other people's lives too much before my nan died,' I said softly, feeling a little self-conscious for telling him. I was thankful that the radio was playing in the background.

'Afterwards, things became quite meaningless for a while and as you know, I stumbled across the café.'

'Like an enchanting butterfly,' he said, smiling. 'You wandered into my life like the daughter I never had and always wanted.'

I was surprised at his words but I knew that I shouldn't interrupt him or he would stop telling me how he felt. It was a new side to James that I was seeing, a softer side.

'You remind me a lot of my late wife.' I looked around to see if anyone was watching us. No one was, Sarah was still writing and Davla was absorbed in her magazine.

'Nina, you have Angie's mannerisms and her inquisitive nature. If you'd asked me if you could carry on staying in my flat, I'd have no hesitation. I'll be honest, I could allow myself to fall in love with you too, if I'd wanted.' He whispered very gently, so that only I heard him say that. I gasped and was at a loss for words.

'You're the first woman I've met since Angie died who I've actually liked. Yet you're a young woman with ambitions of her own and I would never step in the way and for that reason, I chose to see you as the daughter I never had instead.'

He finished speaking and looked at me intently.

'You're a real gentleman, James Hanratty,' I finally said and I felt sad. 'Believe me, there's very few of you around today.'

'Really? You sound like you've only met the bad ones.' He laughed.

'I don't know if they're bad, they just have little understanding.'

***

'Turns out he was in love with you, after all,' Pieter blurted out. 'Wow, he decided to see you as his daughter, instead. He must have been *some* man.' His sarcastic words stung me but I smiled instead.

'He was *some* man,' I said, confidently. 'He really *was*.'

Pieter was speechless. He couldn't believe I was answering back to him. I carried on quickly before an argument began.

***

'Well, it's been over six weeks hasn't it, since I first walked into the café? Since then, I've really learnt to observe people and seen what it is that makes them tick, at least I think I have,' I said to James.

'Ah, so you think you've figured me out. What is it that makes me tick, Nina?' James asked.

'I think it's the memory of your wife and the remembrance of her love.'

'Yes you're right there. She was my pride and joy, God gave me fifteen years with her, the happiest of my life. My only regret was that we never had any children.'

The café became darker, as if James' despair was taking over. It seemed that James retreated into the despair in the café; it draped itself over him like a drunken woman. He closed his eyes and as he sat there absorbed in his world, in his thoughts, I saw a glimmer of something. It was a movement, a flicker, something indefinable, like a match that had been lit briefly in a sea of darkness.

'Memory can tie your heart in knots,' James said, his voice far away.

I sat on the edge of the stool, hardly daring to breath. He was sharing his innermost thoughts with me. He was so different from the James who asked questions at Speakers' Corner or joked with the others in the café. I leaned a little closer gently so that I didn't disturb him.

'Memory can be like a snake coiled at the base of your mind, it reveals itself when it wants to, it will strip away the layers of time, like clothes from a handsome lover,' he continued.

'What does it reveal to you, James?'

'A connection that I never knew I had. I can see the flutter of Angie's dress like a butterfly climbing higher my dear, and her elusive quality becomes real. When I feel her presence that closely, I can bridge the gap between my heart and mind and I feel whole again.'

***

'That is intense,' Pieter interrupted. 'James should have been a poet as well as a philosopher. He was talking to you from his soul, if ever I believed in such a thing, it is now. I don't think I've ever spoken to you on that level. Just tell me Nina, did you have an affair with him?' He sounded desperate.

'Pieter, please, what's gotten into you today? You're getting really insecure over him and I've told you, nothing happened.'

'I'm sorry,' Pieter said, looking down at the table, almost to himself. 'I can't believe how this is making me feel. I feel vulnerable, kind of down about it.'

'I hope not,' I said but he wasn't listening, he was glancing at the café again. The place offered him no solace, so he motioned for me to tell him the rest of my tale.

'Well, it was like James finally dared to face Angela's death completely, realising that he hadn't done that before. A tear found its way to his eye. He wiped it away so roughly, he must have hurt himself.' I said.

'That was the other thing, James believed in another reality, life after death. He felt that Angela was in the midst of everything, but physically, he couldn't touch her or see her, and that was where his grief lay.'

'Did his faith have any impact on you?' Pieter asked.

'You mean did I start believing in life after death?' I said.

'We can safely say you did,' Pieter said, looking at me intensely, his sadness gone.

'Darling, I'm honestly telling you something happened in the café that day. It can only be described as a metaphysical event.'

'What happened?' Pieter asked. He began drinking again.

***

'James' mood was dark. The café responded to it and everything appeared to come to a standstill in the place. Sarah was still at her table and Davla was speaking to a Portuguese girlfriend near the door now,' I said.

'I remember the nights immediately after Angie died and I felt the burden of being alive without her. I knew that her face would never be caressed by my hands again,' James said to me.

***

'It was as if the café opened up the secret to James and I'm not joking, but I thought I was seeing things in there, I thought perhaps I was really tired,' I said and Pieter looked at me intensely.

'What did you see?' Pieter asked, putting his drink down.

'James told me that he saw Angela and she was standing there. He said she was wearing an oriental style shirt covering her slim shoulders and a black silk skirt. And he said she was peering in at us from outside the café,' I said.

'It can't be, he must have been dreaming. Did Davla put something in his coffee, a hallucinogenic perhaps?' Pieter asked.

'I can't explain it but that café was bringing Angela back to life again,' I said.

'How is that possible?' Pieter asked, nervously.

***

'James and I looked outside the window and I saw a woman standing near Davla and her friend. Her frame was in the doorway and she had one sandaled foot poised inside. She was as real as you are here now before me and at first I thought it was another friend of theirs,' I said.

***

'You're telling me that you saw her ghost?' Pieter asked, his face looked pale, his eyes widened.

'She looked just like the woman in the photos in James' flat. Even Davla and her friend stopped for a moment as if they'd been disturbed. A chill had crept into the café, a feeling of anticipation that reminded me of a dog I'd once seen barking furiously at an empty room.

'I'm telling you, James was willing her back to life again, he was recreating her and we all felt it. It was suddenly cold in the café and Sarah put her jacket on. James got off his stool and walked towards the door. He hesitated near it and then came back quickly and sat down again and in that instant it became warmer in the place.'

'So you really did *see* Angela? Fuck, I can't believe it.' Pieter sunk back into his chair.

'Yes but it was brief. I saw her and I definitely *felt* her.'

***

'That was the strangest thing,' James said, looking at me. 'I thought, well, sounds silly but I thought of Angie as if she were with us somehow.'

'I thought I saw someone standing near Davla too,' I said. I had a throbbing headache.

'So did I,' James said, he grabbed my arm lightly and Sarah looked up. We smiled at each other and she went back to reading what she'd written.

James was willing me to say more. He wanted to know that I'd seen her, but I was too frightened, I wasn't sure what was going on and I felt queasy.

I put my arm on James' shoulder and told him to calm down. I said I felt funny and was probably getting ill. He kept asking me if I'd seen Angela.

'My imagination must have run away with me,' I said to James. 'For a moment I thought I did, but I'm sure I was mistaken.'

***

'I'm sure your imagination did run away with you,' Pieter said. 'Or how else do I explain all this to my family?'

'This story is for you, not for your family,' I said, firmly. 'Why are you worried about them?'

'They will never believe me,' Pieter said, shaking his head. 'I don't know, Nina. Reading peoples' thoughts in the café, a Buddhist temple emerging from nowhere and now ghostly wives. What will they think about it all? I've lost you in your story.'

'I'm sorry you feel that way,' I said. 'This is not about you or me.'

'But you must finish,' Pieter urged me on. 'What happened to James? Honestly, the next thing I know the café will just disappear into thin air.'

'Maybe you're right there.' I smiled.

***

James was disappointed with me and the look on his face said it all. I felt terrible and my head kept pounding like mad. He finally told me that he would see me back at home. He grabbed his satchel roughly. He was so determined to leave that he rushed past Davla, breaking up her conversation and leaving her to respond furiously in Portuguese. I watched him until I could no longer see him.

I was relieved he'd left because I knew I'd seen Angela and now I thought I was going crazy. It was as if the café had been creating her again because James was so sad. I suppose seeing her had shocked me and made me realise that there was another reality, I'd just witnessed it. My nan had been right all along. I did have the gift, as she called it. I was spiritually awake now and able to see people who had passed over. Davla's friend left shortly afterwards and the atmosphere in the café became lighter, but the pain in my head stayed with me all day.

CHAPTER FOURTEEN

'Did you and James have an argument?' Davla asked.

She had seen him rush past, intent on escaping from the café. I realised she had no idea what James was going through, so I shook my head and she went outside to clean the tables.

'Sarah, you've been writing all afternoon, are you writing a book?' I asked.

Sarah smiled. 'Hardly, Nina it's just a letter to my son, although he might not even read it as we don't have the best relationship.'

She took an envelope out of her bag and folded the letter in it. Davla came over towards us, her heels hitting the ground fast.

'My dad's just called and my mother's really upset because of her friend's funeral. Dad's asked me to go and check up on her. He can't be there because he's in a long meeting all day.' She paused.

'I thought things were difficult with you both, it's unfair to expect you to go,' I said.

'Yes, but it'd be *worse* if I didn't. It's no problem, Eric is on his way, he'll be here in five.' Davla sighed.

She grabbed her bag and looked around anxiously for her keys. Within a few minutes she was gone and by the time Eric came in, Sarah and I were sitting together at her table drinking coffee.

'You two look cosy,' he said warmly.

He came over and sat with us. The café was quiet and we could hear the sounds of the street outside.

Sarah held the letter gingerly in her hand, afraid that it might snap in two.

'Is that a personal letter Sarah? You seem to be guarding it with your life,' Eric observed.

'As I told Nina, it's for my son and he won't read it.'

'Why not? You took the time to write it.'

Sarah nodded sadly. 'He's being influenced by his dad and I'm in everyone's bad books because I don't like my former husband's new girlfriend. She's about thirty-five and looks like a glamour model.'

'She sounds like a bitch,' Eric said and Sarah looked up.

'Eric, you're right. She's a *total* bitch.'

'That was the moment when we broke the ice with Sarah, when she started to open up to us. Up to that point, she was just one of the people in the café who remained an enigma to me. She was intelligent and educated and knew a lot about her Jewish culture.'

***

'It's odd a woman her age going out so much as if she's in her twenties. It's as if she has no peace,' Pieter said suddenly.

'Sarah was very restless, for sure. A few weeks earlier, she'd told me a bit about herself. She'd been part of a Zionist youth club in her younger days and it was where she met her husband. She loved music too, in particular Jazz. She also went to Art gallery openings and sometimes James and Tony went with her.'

'So she always had someone with her?' Pieter asked.

'Mostly, although I sometimes saw people stare at her oddly, an older woman dancing to music, swaying her hips barefoot on the grass in Soho Square. The thing is she didn't care; she had a funny way of swaying her arms as if her life depended on it.'

'I wouldn't even hang around with people like that,' Pieter remarked.

'You say that but Sarah's ability to talk to anyone on the streets always impressed me. She was a natural communicator, she would start by talking to the musicians, then the organisers and eventually other people on the benches, tourists, anyone who cared to listen. Eventually, some would become irritated, but the musicians were never rude to her. She had a genuine appreciation of different musical styles.

'However, I think the reality was that she was always an outsider to their world, as if she were rubbing a window to clean the dirt off to try and get a closer look at what was on the other side.

'It was difficult to say what Sarah was about and I wouldn't have even realised if the café hadn't given me the insight. When Davla left, the energy in the café shifted and I felt as if my nan were sitting beside us. I kept thinking I was smelling sandalwood like the incense she used to light,' I said.

'You really felt your grandma beside you?' Pieter asked, his face clouded with doubt.

'Yes, she was there because she wanted to show me what Sarah was going through,' I said. 'I saw that something was troubling her deeply and it was like she was on the edge of a precarious cliff waiting to fall, with the sound of the waves crashing all around.'

***

'You know I rise alone every morning and discover that I have to face the rest of the day alone without any family,' Sarah said.

'Where are they?' Eric asked.

'They're just gone.'

'I have too many bad memories and on the days when those memories come to life, they seem to itch like mad. They beat like a fast rhythm. Those beats pierce my soul, *boom, boom, boom*. It never ends, it only gets worse,' Sarah said.

***

'What was that itch she had, some kind of disease?' Pieter laughed.

'Stop it, she meant she had a terrible restlessness,' I said. I was annoyed at him but I kept my temper intact.

***

'Lately it's like having a whole tribe of African drummers weaving their music in my mind and I can't rest because of it. Even when I sleep, they hammer away, so that when I get up; when I should feel energetic, I only feel the sadness they create and there is only the bleakness of facing another day,' Sarah continued.

'That sounds crazy,' Eric said. 'Have you thought about visiting a therapist, Sarah?'

'I don't need a therapist, unless he can heal my heart,' Sarah said sharply.

The evening was approaching fast and Sarah acted in an uncharacteristic manner and she began to tell us about herself.

Outside it was beginning to rain, slowly at first and then fiercely, so that the rain ran in sheets across the windows of the café.

'When I was a young child growing up in Farnborough, I was relatively happy and we were a wealthy Jewish family.

'There was only my brother and me. My parents spoiled us. At high school, I discovered boys and that was fun.'

Sarah tapped my arm playfully.

'I never had sex with anyone,' she added quickly. 'I wasn't like that but I still think that I was wild for that time. It wasn't heard of in my cultural circles to flirt around as I did.

'I met David, that's my ex-husband in that Zionist Club, I was only twenty two. We began to see each other and fell in love eventually. I was always told by my parents that marriage was everything. So that's thirty years of married life and of duty to family and friends. It was what young Jewish women waited for and cherished, it was everything. Yet now I feel like I'm a building that's been demolished. I'm just a bit of rubble now.

'On the surface I seem placid enough, but it feels like a large rock has been dropped into the centre of a small lake. The ripples caused have made contact with the heart of the matter. It's my heart that has fallen, that hasn't survived. I've done so well to conceal it, so well that

I've almost forgotten about it myself. I realise though that I can't truly hide something that contains so much love,' Sarah said.

'That must have been very painful,' Eric said.

'My dreams of an idyllic family were crushed. My husband was a violent man and his tempers were unpredictable. I can remember clearly when the violence really started. It was during my first pregnancy, in the early stages. He had slapped my face really hard,' Sarah said.

***

'I started to get upset as I was thinking about how my father had slapped my mother in front of me because she hadn't cooked the dinner on time. I'd walked over to him and shouted at him to stop and he'd just stared at me, his eyes bloodshot,' I told Pieter.

'That's not a nice thing to remember,' Pieter said.

'It all came back as I spoke to Sarah and I remembered my father's need to lash out and his target was my mother,' I said.

***

'The shock of it doesn't register in your mind until a lot later,' Sarah said. 'You tell yourself all kinds of things, that it's a one off and he didn't mean it, that you love him and he loves you. It's crazy Nina, I think us women live in a fairy tale world sometimes.

'It was too late when the children were born and my world became narrower. David had an edge of hate in him that was constantly alive. No one else saw it. Even the children only did occasionally when they heard his shouting. He hated the way I laughed, even when the laughter gradually became hollow, like mist dissolving fast. I never knew the reason for his anger. Only that it lived in him, caged up, and that it sought release now and again.'

Her eyes looked vacant and I felt my own anger towards my father rise in me again like a wave of nausea.

Eric was quietly listening to us both, his face thoughtful.

'The anger drove David to hold a knife to my throat once. He ignored the children and let them cry loudly in a separate room. I lost consciousness at the foot of the stairs, after he kicked me down.

'When I came around, I was in a hospital bed and one of my ribs was broken. My left eye was glued together and my ankle was swollen. My youngest son was only ten and he had managed to call an ambulance, otherwise I don't know what would have happened to me.'

***

'That's disgusting,' Pieter said, loudly. 'The bastard should have been locked up. Did she report him to the police?'

'David lied to her family and friends claiming that she had fallen after tripping over one of the children's toys on the stairs. His story was met with disbelief, but people remained quiet. Nobody interfered at this point; it was only later, when the children were older, that the whispers started in their social circles,' I said.

'I still don't get why she didn't call the police,' Pieter said incredulously.

'Frankly, neither do I,' I said.

***

'People looked at me with pity at the Synagogues and yet, they did nothing,' Sarah went on. 'One friend said if I was in trouble – that's what she called it – I should leave my husband. The children had grown up right in the midst of the turmoil and whatever damage was going to affect them had already happened,' Sarah said and she wiped tears from her eyes.

Eric handed her a tissue and patted her arm.

'I'm sorry Sarah, that all sounds terrible,' he said.

'It was, believe me. I was violated against, mentally, physically and spiritually.'

She was looking at the rain outside the window. I was so absorbed with her story, that I noticed nothing else.

'Eventually, my social circle broke up, and I lost contact with all my friends. No one ever called again and my whole Jewish world collapsed. The worst was yet to come; when my children became teenagers, they turned against me because David brainwashed them, it was that simple,' Sarah said.

'My God Sarah, your world fell apart really fast,' Eric said.

'Like the speed of lightning, Eric. My children, the love and meaning of my life were slipping away from me, faster than I could have ever imagined. The distance between us grew until it seemed to encompass the earth twice over.'

We were silent for a moment and there was an air of isolation in the café.

'I'm terrified of being alone,' Sarah said as if she felt it too.

'Tell me, Nina, after your dad hit your mother could you ever forgive him?'

'I don't think I can right now. The violence created a huge divide between him and my mother. I don't know if I can ever repair it,' I answered.

'So now imagine years of that, forgiveness isn't a word in my dictionary,' Sarah said.

Eric lent forward and picked up Sarah's hands delicately in his.

'You know Sarah, you've found the one person you've never really paid any attention to and that's yourself. You've got a loving heart and you only show it occasionally, it's like you've learnt to hide it pretty much permanently. It's like a clap of thunder you only hear in the distance that reverberates into the mighty universe. It's never forgotten Sarah, it's out there somewhere, you must bring it back.'

Sarah was crying and Eric squeezed her hands.

'According to David, my daughter never wants to see me again. I feel like shouting at her. When I'm dead and gone, will anything change? Will she realise what I meant to her then?' Sarah asked.

***

'After she said that, an anguished look came upon her face, it was the heart of the matter. Her daughter was the one thing that had created all those ripples, the single event that had sent her heart into hiding,' I told Pieter.

He didn't say anything, so I continued.

'Sarah just hung her head over the table and she looked so fragile that I wanted to rip her away from that place. I wanted to take her back to that time where she was happy with her daughter again. Where the drums stopped beating and the whisperings and longings of yesterday didn't stoop to remind her that all was lost.'

'Wasn't there anything you could do to help her?' Pieter asked.

'What could I possibly do? Even Eric offered advice, but we couldn't change anything,' I said.

***

Maybe I never lived for myself. Firstly I was the child of my parents. Afterwards, I was the parent of my children, so who on earth am I?

I could hear Sarah's thoughts and in the midst of them, it settled. Like a gentle whisper on the eve of a storm, a warning of the turbulence to come, I saw it again. It was a butterfly on the crest of a wave with its wings fluttering loosely.

'I'm the one who's old and who should be dead. But in reality my daughter is the one who's died,' Sarah whispered.

A butterfly caught in the storm that was coming in from the ocean, trapped by the force of it. It wasn't supposed to survive for too long, that was its fate. Yet it still left its mark before it departed and it reminded us that there was something extraordinary in life.

The movement of the butterfly's wings lifted gracefully.

'Eric, you're right. The only thing I have left to live for now, is me, Sarah,' she said.

The butterfly rose higher and higher. Its wings moved up and down several times before it was gone. The waves crashed into Sarah's world and the incoming storm and the blackness of the sea raged upon everything.

The rain outside was lightening now. Eric smiled at me, his eyes holding mine for a second.

Sarah wiped her face quickly. She was placing her heart back where even she would have trouble finding it. It was no longer of any use to her because she couldn't bear to look at it for too long. It now had to go back to the place where the darkness took over, where a jewel lay undiscovered again.

'Maybe I've told you too much today,' she said, looking at us both.

'You told us what you had to,' Eric said. 'It's nothing to be ashamed about. It reminds me of how life can change so rapidly and be so fragile, like a butterfly.'

I looked at him but he was giving Sarah a big hug. He sat down on his stool again afterwards and winked at me.

It was clear that Sarah had her guard up again. Now that her heart was back underwater, vanishing into the depths. As she kissed us goodnight and walked away from the café, every step she took away from us, her heart kept sinking like a dead flower, floating to the bottom of the murky lake. It was back in position again, where no one would ever discover it.

CHAPTER FIFTEEN

There was a shift in the weather the day after Eric and I saw Sarah and the café looked gloomy under a grey sky. I was drinking coffee with James. He was sitting across from me, absorbed in the morning newspapers.

It was early morning and Eric was unloading crates of deliveries from a small van.

I hadn't slept too well, my mind racing with the possibility of working abroad. As usual, James was up earlier than me. He'd become quieter lately, like the unsettling silence after a storm.

Eric placed a plate of hot fresh croissants on the table and smiled at me. Davla looked tired as if she'd been up late. She was busy preparing fresh coffee, grinding it and putting it in glass jars.

'Hi darling, how are you?' She was in a good mood and wore a beautiful yellow flowing dress. Her hair was tied back and she had hardly any make up on, it made her look younger.

It was still warm and yet the wind blew just a little more than it had in the previous days. The summer was beginning to ebb away, like a tide that had been in too long and was now leaving, littering the beach with its strewn possessions. The café, like the beach, contained the remnants of a revealing summer. There were secrets that had been shared by a few people. These were now there waiting to be understood, like precious and colourful shells that lay on the shore.

James reached for a croissant and ate it at an alarming speed. He peered over at me.

'Are you expecting a phone call? You keep looking anxiously at your phone.'

'Yes, from Amsterdam. I might be going there to work in October. I've applied for a couple of good jobs and been told I've been short-listed for one.'

'That's wonderful, my dear.'

He didn't sound convincing.

'Just let me know so that I can start looking for a new tenant.'

'James, I *don't* actually have a job yet. If I did you'd be the first to know.'

A flash of hurt crossed his eyes for the briefest of moments, but he said nothing.

'I'm sorry if I've upset you about my possible move,' I said gently.

'It's okay, dear,' he said and smiled. 'We agreed something like that anyway, didn't we? It's just that,' he paused and wiped his brow with his handkerchief. 'Well, the summer has *flown* past and it's almost over, like the blink of an eye. Don't you think so?'

'I suppose so, but it's not *quite* over.'

'The point is Nina,' he began, and his now familiar teacher voice took over. 'It's always the good times that speed past. It's the annoying stuff that lingers. Anyway, I don't know if I'm going to get another tenant. Maybe I'll spend some time alone, just being by myself, contemplating life.'

'James, you do that already, too much of it is bad,' I laughed.

'Tell me about it,' he chuckled. 'I don't want to end up like some of those crazies in Speakers' Corner who stand alone on their crates, and nobody, and I *mean bloody nobody* wants anything to do with them.'

I wondered if he'd had an argument with someone at Speakers' Corner.

Eric came over to us. He was wearing pale blue jeans with fluorescent blue flip flops and his yellow palm trees T-shirt.

'Is it another day out of the office?' James asked.

'Yes, they owe me a lot time off,' Eric explained.

'And so you come here instead? Davla tells us it's terrible in this place,' James laughed.

Eric smiled. 'That's her experience, I like the vibe here.'

Davla came over with a tray of fresh coffee for everyone.

'We were here until three yesterday morning, going through all the pros and cons of why I should close this place down and go back to Brazil,' she said.

'What did you decide?' I asked.

'Let's just say things got a little emotional,' Eric said.

'Eric thinks I should stay here for another year and make this place work. It's too long for me and I want to go back home, so we had a silly argument and nothing was resolved.'

'We even took into account everyone who is a regular in the café, from James to Sarah and even you got a mention!' Eric said, putting his arm around me.

'Me?' I said and they both laughed at my surprise.

'Even you, babe, we thought it was great that you kept coming back here as if this place were special somehow.'

'Like it or not, you're one of us now,' Davla said. 'We're like family and you do intrigue me, Nina. There is something different about you but I don't really know you that well. None of us do really.'

She looked at Eric.

'What she means is, babe, is *just what are you all about?* It's like you landed from outer space, you invaded our world, and soon you'll be gone and we'll be none the wiser. We know so little about you love,' Eric said, gently.

He looked at me and in his expression I knew that he did know me really. He was saying it for the benefit of Davla, who apart from the conversation I'd had about my father, had no clue about me.

Does she just find it hard to talk about herself?

I heard Davla's thought pass through the café, she was looking at me as she sipped her coffee. The thoughts that circled the air in the café didn't startle me anymore like they used to. The café was a friend to me now and I knew that the time would come very soon when I would have to leave it and that was the very thing that I had learnt from it, that nothing stays the same forever.

A hush ensued into the depths of the café and it seemed as if our world at that moment was only the surrounding walls of the place.

'I feel that you will go soon and God only knows if you'll be back. I'm sure the others will agree that we would like to remember you with fondness, not just as another customer who dragged herself in here one sunny day,' James chipped in.

He paused and it seemed as if he had the atmosphere of the whole café in his hand at that moment. It was a ball of extraordinary colours that James seemed to have glowing in his palm, a present from the café. He was holding it tenderly and it was like he was holding gold and silver droplets in his hands from another world, flecks of time and memory, beauty and sadness. Eric and Davla were transfixed by his words.

'It would be great for us if you left something of yourself here for us to remember you by, a hook if you like. Perhaps you could just tell us something wonderful today, that would help us to really see who you *are*.'

James finished speaking, and put his hands on the table as if signifying the end of his speech. The café was adrift with his words, they floated in the air like silver and gold feathers that brushed our cheeks and fell into our hair.

Eric and I looked at each other at the same time and the secret knowledge of the café that we shared passed between us.

'I can tell you about this time when we went to visit my nan in India, when I was about ten years old,' I began and I felt vulnerable, as it was the first time I'd spoken at length about her with them.

***

'Let me get this straight,' Pieter's words cut into my story. 'So you shared a secret story from your childhood with a bunch of strangers, something you've never done with me.' He said it quietly, as if he'd almost given up the fight.

'I'm telling you now,' I said calmly. 'If I can go on, that would be great. You see, there is this seed that my nan had sown into the depths of my mind when I was a young girl and it resulted in the blossoming of an understanding that has stood the test of time. That tree is now fully grown and it stands like a solitary landmark against the weathering of the years.'

***

'It was a warm October day in old Delhi and I was only ten years old. It was early morning, and the sounds of the birds filled the air, like a lively orchestra, accompanied by the shouting men selling their vegetables and fruit, rolling their carts past the houses and the early morning traffic.

'I was with nan and we were alone because my parents had gone shopping early in the big bustling bazaars in old Delhi. We had arrived a week earlier and every day had been packed visiting relatives and friends.

'My nan said she wanted to show me something. She was excited about it and said they were letters written to her from my grandfather, secret love letters. It was a chance to find out more about this romantic man whom I'd never met. He had died two years before my birth.

'So I followed her, as she led me towards the box room on the second floor of the house. It was the family store room really and for me, a young girl of ten, it was steeped in mystery. Nan opened the rusty lock with a big sigh and I followed her into the room. It was dark and there was a musty smell. She switched the light on and the single bulb dimly lit the room.

'Nan showed me her wedding dress and afterwards, she said she wanted to show me what she called her box of memories. There seemed to be suitcases and boxes piled up above my head on thick shelves. I couldn't imagine how anyone had put them there, until I noticed the wooden ladder folded against the wall, lying silently like a witness to the many memories stored in the room. It was dusty in there and I sneezed several times in a row.

'Nan picked up her ladder gingerly as the box was on the third shelf. I held onto the bottom rung for dear life, worried in case she fell. Her hand brushed the top of the two suitcases piled on top of each other and she fumbled across the top, not seeing what she was looking for. When she finally located it, she gave a little shout of delight. It was a slim white box.

'She climbed down slowly, holding it in her left hand carefully. When she reached the floor, I was disappointed, because the box seemed so small.

'She sat down on the chair in the corner of the room and I saw that the box had two handles cut out on either side. She opened the lid, and then it gave way all of a sudden and flew open, like a secret box that wanted to reveal all of its contents in a hurry.

'I screamed as something flew out of it and spun towards the ceiling. I thought it was a bat and it was going to bite me, so I ran towards the open door. Nan called me and said it was only a moth, although the biggest she'd ever seen.'

'I don't know how it managed to get in there,' she said.

'I dared to look up behind me and there it was hovering near the bulb. As the room seemed so high, I craned my neck to look at it, and once I did, I was taken over by the magnificence of it.'

'It's a butterfly, not a moth,' I said, getting excited.

'She wasn't listening to me, she was holding crumpled envelopes, trying to make sense of the letters in them.

'The butterfly was big and it was beating its wings furiously close to the light, as if our disturbing it had made it mad somehow. It cast a huge shadow on the wall behind where nan was sitting, and to me, the shadow seemed like a huge monster above her head. She weaved her hand through piles of love letters and the threads of time that had passed already.'

'I can still see it now,' I said as the yellow of Davla's dress mingled with the ebony of Eric's skin and the blue of James' eyes.

'I could still see the delicate wings as the butterfly eventually descended, close to nan. She looked up at me and laughed at me standing there watching it. I couldn't take my eyes of it. It had hypnotised me and I can still see it now, as I did all those years ago.

'I remember vividly that it appeared to be dancing, the enchanting movements of the wing, up and down, were holding a secret unto themselves. It was dancing around Nan's head and never once did she push it away.

'The butterfly changed direction after a moment and I darted and squealed as it came towards me and then flew out of the door. It seemed to me that it had an agenda of its own, as if it were following an invisible source from where it had come. I ran after it, as it carried on flying up and down into the hallway and through the open door onto the small balcony, where my nan sometimes sat to read her books.

'I could see the sky above us. A floor higher was the roof from which I had viewed the surrounding area with nan and the sky seemed infinite from there.

'As I recall the wondrous colours of that butterfly in all of its glory, it was a rich red colour and it was black at the tips of the wings. The small black body stood out and it had a few white and yellow spots at the bottom of each wing.

'It hovered directly above me, as if it sensed that it was being watched and it seemed to do a little dance for me, its wings fluttering.

'I wanted to reach out and capture it for myself, but something stopped me. I knew that I shouldn't do that and instead it seemed to me that the butterfly was letting me see it in all its glory. The rhythm with which its wings fluttered, the gentle grace with which it swayed in the air, like a tiny trapeze artist was all for me. I told myself that I was the lone witness to the magic of it all.

'It soon took off, rising gently in the air, like a puff of smoke. It flew up into the blue sky that was visible to my outstretched neck and as I watched it swayed from left to right, until the shape was no longer visible as a butterfly anymore. It was only a red dot, a piece of confetti thrown into the air, colouring a vast sky with a delicate smudge of red.'

***

'So that's where your fascination with butterflies comes from,' Pieter said. 'From a little girl's imagination.'

'From a little girl's experience,' I corrected him.

'I can see that something special happened,' Pieter said. 'But I'm afraid that I don't completely see the magic of it.'

'I thought you'd understand,' I said, sadly.

'Hell, let's get more wine,' Pieter said. 'We may as well enjoy our last night before we get back to Amsterdam tomorrow and everything falls apart.' He smirked at me.

'I think you've had enough,' I said angrily. He ignored me and called the waitress over to order another bottle.

'Come on Nina, what happened?' Pieter asked. 'Hurry up and tell me before I get too pissed to remember.'

I ignored him and continued.

***

'I was talking about that experience when I was ten. Living with James had made me realise how Angela's death had impacted every part of his life and it was the same for Davla's difficult relationship with her mother and Sarah's grief for her daughter. It was all part of our pain, our journey, our sadness. We mixed happier memories into them to carry us through. They were as fragile and as beautiful as the butterfly as it escaped that day.

'We all lived with our joys and sorrows; they were different sides of the same coin. We lived with everything intact as we understood it and it was only when a significant event shook our lives, until the butterfly lifted away from the memories, that the movement of our lives changed, like a stream that abruptly has to alter its course. The stream that carries it forward is the water of experience and it twists and turns. And in that change, we go along with it into a new direction, which brings with it greater clarity.

'Everyone in the café shared in the bittersweet sides of the coin, the fragility and beauty of being alive, and this movement became the butterfly dance. It was James dancing in his room, wearing the dervish's clothes, it was Sarah's heart plunging into the depths of despair and it was the fleeting kiss between Davla and Eric. And it was inescapable this dance, it made us animated and flirty, yet sad, lonely and full of despair too sometimes. The vastness of it all was frightening and elusive, like the butterfly that escaped into the limitless blue sky. That was the best day I ever had with nan,' I said. 'Afterwards, she read her private letters to me. They were sent by my grandfather after they married at times when they were apart because he travelled a lot as his family lived in the South of India.'

***

'In other words, that butterfly was sitting on your grandfather's love letters to your grandmother, holding those memories, until it was released. Goodness Nina, I didn't realise you were so sentimental,' James said.

He looked at me tenderly as if he were proud of me and smiled.

I was surprised at my tears when Eric put his arm around me.

'This is your personal journey. Somewhere along the line, as I've told you before, you decided you wanted to know the true reality of life,' Eric said.

'So this is it? It's a lovely memory but I miss her so much.'

'Listen Nina, no one has it easy in this life, let me tell you, *no one*. Painful as it may be, it's still a treasure,' Eric said.

'I returned to nan that day with the strangest feeling that I had lost something valuable and she saw my glum expression and told me that we are not meant to keep everything in this life, that the butterfly would have died if I had captured it, she said nothing lasts forever.

I started crying so she put me on her knee and read me the letters from my grandfather, translating them from Hindi into English and I eventually feel asleep.'

'That's simply beautiful, Nina. As soon as you get a job, I will throw you a party here to celebrate, you have my word,' Davla said. She disappeared to the back of the café to make some breakfast.

'A party would be great, a good way to remember this place and us, of course,' James said and his words were tinged with sadness.

At that moment, my mobile started to ring.

I rushed off my seat, grabbing my phone.

'It's from Amsterdam, from that company.'

I couldn't talk properly with everyone looking at me, so I walked a little way outside the café and turned into Shaftesbury Avenue.

James stopped as soon as he saw me walk in. His face was expectant, as if he were waiting for me to break the news.

'And?' he asked; his voice thick with emotion.

Eric was helping Davla stack some books on the shelf. He saw me in the mirror and stopped, turning to look at me.

'Did you get an interview? Don't keep me in suspense any longer, I'm not young anymore, I might not be able to take it,' James said.

Everyone laughed.

My face must have given it all away, I felt exuberant.

'Yes, I have an interview for a job with an American media company based in Amsterdam. They want to speak to me in a day or two, isn't that bloody great?'

Eric clapped loudly.

'Babe, I knew you could do it!'

'Fantastic, they obviously move faster on the continent than they do here,' Davla said.

I was thankful for their words of encouragement, but it was James I was worried about. Dear James, my friend, the teacher, the philosopher, it was as if the thought of going away suddenly became a reality and another door was opening up for me.

He sat there quietly on his stool, as if his world had just come to an end. He looked so disheartened that I kept thinking of the old statue that was precious yet invisible now, the one that nobody noticed anymore.

'Congratulations, my dear,' he said, but his heart wasn't in it. In the short space of time that we'd become friends in, he probably felt I was about to pull that rug from under his feet, crush the new found understanding we had just built. Until nothing was left but a pile of gravel and dust, and bare loneliness, underneath it all like an unwelcome discovery. And it made me wish that I'd never told them.

CHAPTER SIXTEEN

My interview took place the next day during a conference call from Amsterdam in which two other members of the team were also involved.

***

'I tried to call you to let you know how it went,' I said to Pieter.

'I remember that you left a message for me,' Pieter said. 'So, that was the beginning of your life as you know it now.'

'Yes, the start of the journey towards Amsterdam,' I said. 'The start of getting married and…' I paused.

Pieter looked at me anxiously, waiting for a response but I said nothing. Instead, I continued with my narrative.

***

It was mid-morning, James and I were sitting in the living room and I was answering the questions that Mr Klute, the interviewer, was asking me. They were impressed by my past experience, especially the work that I had done with disadvantaged groups in the community.

James pretended to be reading the newspaper but he appeared to be reading the same page over and over, and I realised he was listening to what I was saying.

Mr Klute asked me why I hadn't been working for a while. I didn't mention nan's death, instead I told them why after three years I'd left my last job. I said that I'd needed time to re-evaluate my options, including the possibility of working abroad.

'You have an excellent reference from your previous role,' Mr Klute said. 'It's not usual for us to interview people over the phone. However, we decided to make an exception in your case.'

I thanked him and he said that they had two other people to interview shortly and would let me know their decision by early evening.

'I felt elated as if I'd broken through something significant that day,' I said.

'That sounds very positive and I've got a good feeling about this job,' James said, putting the newspaper down and peering at me from behind his glasses.

'They like me and they've never even met me.'

'You seem to have that effect,' James said affectionately.

'If it upsets you, we don't have to talk about it,' I said.

James laughed and waved his hand dismissively.

'It's nothing like that, dear. I'm not going to be selfish about this and I've been thinking about it this morning and realised I have nothing to be sad about, it's been a delight to have you in my life, short though it was.'

'You looked sad yesterday,' I reminded him.

'That was yesterday, it's another day now. I've learnt a lot from you especially about Angie. I don't think I faced her death for a really long time. I mean do you really think I didn't *feel* it, for so long?'

'James, only you can answer that.'

'Yes, you're right. I think I did push it away to the back of my mind, thank you Nina.'

'For what?'

'For helping me bring her back, for feeling her love again.'

He came and sat next to me on the sofa.

'I'm not sure I did anything,' I said.

'Yes, you did. It's your presence, you're like her. You did it unwittingly and so you were sent to me for a reason. I always suspected that, even the first time I met you in the café with Davla.'

'James, you're totally confusing me.'

He laughed and grabbed my hand in a friendly way and shook it gently.

'Everything happens for a reason, my dear. Someone above sent you into my life. Who knows? It might have even been her, I really believe that. I was suffering and sometimes I *still* suffer because I remember her. You came to stay with me and woke me up, out of my stupor,' James said.

'Well, thanks James, but I don't get you.'

'Never mind, one day you will. As I've told you before, you're the butterfly that flew into my life to remind me that life goes on.'

'You're speaking in metaphors and anyway, you're a Christian, they don't believe in all that airy fairy stuff.'

'Says who? I believe God can remind us all in ways we understand, who on earth can judge that?'

'No one, I guess,' I said.

I sat there, relieved that he felt happier.

'Funny thing that! I suppose memories are the essence of who we are really. Come on, let's head to the café and I'll buy you lunch to celebrate,' James said.

'Celebrate?'

'A great interview and I'm sure a job.' He smiled as he grabbed his satchel and keys.

***

'James had eyes for you only,' Pieter said, pouring himself another glass of wine from a new bottle. He thanked the waitress and poured some into my glass.

'Cheers, Nina,' he said. 'To new beginnings.'

I clinked my glass with his. 'New beginnings,' I whispered. 'What do you mean by that, exactly?'

Pieter shrugged. 'Just new beginnings, nothing untoward.'

I felt sad watching him drink one glass of wine after another. The story of the café felt like a life raft to hold on, as my emotions about my marriage drifted on a huge ocean.

***

There was a big lunch-time crowd at the café and we had to wait almost half an hour to be served. Davla was snowed under with requests for sandwiches, fresh juices, chicken and brie when as if on cue, Eric arrived to help. It was almost three in the afternoon by the time the rush subsided and Eric and Davla had cleared the tables.

In a few minutes, the café was clean again and Davla sat down on the table close to the door, flicking idly through the latest edition of *Elle* with a steaming cup of coffee. She picked up the tarot cards next to her and handed them to me.

'Come on, Nina, shuffle. Let's see what's happening in your zone now you've done this interview.'

'You did it already?' Eric asked.

'This morning and they'll let me know tonight.'

He whistled. 'Boy, they work fast on the continent.'

She turned it over slowly and looked at it.

'I knew it.'

'Which one is it?' She took my palm and handed me the eight of pentacles card.

It was a picture of a man holding a hammer in his raised right arm, preparing to bring it down on a huge coin, the size of a plate. He wore a red hat and a protective brown cloth, like an apron covering his blue clothes. Other tools lay around him and seven large golden coins that he had already made were lined up in a row against the table.

'Working hard for your money, babe, this job is as good as yours, that's what the card is saying. Pentacles are about money and I'd say it's a new time to be creative. Looks like good money too.'

'I'll believe that when they tell me I've got it,' I said.

'What's wrong with you? You've come here and built all this faith in yourself and understood others, your words, not mine, I should say. And you don't think you'll get the job? Nina, believe it, really *believe* it!' Eric said and I was surprised at his strong words.

'He's absolutely right young lady,' James said. 'Honestly, I can see myself having one of those readings before long,' he said, laughing.

'I'll really have to see that to believe that,' Davla said.

She raised her eyebrows at Eric but he was watching me and James as if he'd had a sudden realisation about us both and an understanding crossed his face. He knew that we had built up a friendship that could only be born of living in James' flat. It was one of sharing in James' ideas about Rasputin and the world, religion and love over numerous cups of tea. It was observing the shrine to Angela that dominated his living room and listening to the beautiful memories of his wife as they flooded the flat.

Sarah and Tony stepped into the café together.

Sarah was wearing a pale yellow dress fitted with a thin gold belt at the waist. Over her neck, she'd thrown a see through gold scarf, fastened on her left shoulder by a brooch of a leopard with green stones for its eyes. Her hair was tied back in a ponytail, scraped off her face neatly as if she'd combed it carefully into place. A pale pink colour shimmered on her lips and her cheeks were lightly rouged, she looked elegant.

They both came over to us straight away and sat down.

'You both should be ashamed of yourselves,' Sarah said, in a jesting manner to me and James. 'You missed the last of this summer's music this lunchtime in Trafalgar Square and it was fantastic.'

'I don't know about the music but you look fabulous,' James said and Sarah looked pleased.

***

'At that moment, my phone rang and at first I thought it was you because it was an international code, then I realised it was Mr

Klute and my heart started pounding and I felt really nervous,' I said to Pieter. 'It was too noisy in the café, so I stepped outside under James' watchful eyes and walked around the corner into Shaftesbury Avenue again.'

'We'd like to offer you the job, we think you would be an excellent candidate,' Mr Klute had said, or words to that effect.

'I remember thanking him and he must have heard the excitement in my voice because he laughed and told me they would send the contract by email and I needed to sign it and send it back,' I continued. 'After I'd hung up, I stood transfixed in Shaftesbury Avenue for a few minutes, my head spinning. I realised that within the space of another few weeks, my life would drastically change. I called my mother and told her and she was delighted for me and asked me to stop by for dinner before I went to Amsterdam.

'I also called you and got through straight away because I was praying that you'd be in and thankfully, when I heard your voice I couldn't help but shout down the phone.'

'*I got the fucking job!* I think that's what you shouted, it was very funny,' Pieter said. He smiled and for the briefest of moments, I saw the man I had fallen in love with once more.

I smiled as I continued with my story.

***

I went back to the café to tell the others. Nobody saw me come in, Sarah was talking to James and Davla and Eric were behind the counter, with their backs towards me.

I felt a little awkward for coming back and I wasn't sure if I was making too much of a big deal about it all, when Eric turned around and our eyes locked.

'Did you or did you not? That is the question,' he asked gently and I knew he knew the answer before I'd even spoken.

'Of course I did,' I said.

'That's fantastic, babe,' he said. He came over and hugged me. In his enthusiasm he lifted me off my feet.

'Whoa there, be careful,' James said, coming up behind me.

'The cards never lie,' Davla said and a look of envy crossed her face.

Wouldn't I love to be in your shoes, leaving this place behind.

Her troubled thought came over to me but I was beyond its reach now.

'We need to organise that party,' James said to me.

Davla was opening a bottle of wine to celebrate and Sarah passed a glass to everyone. Later, Davla lit all the candles on the newly polished tables.

Eric was humming along softly to Stevie Wonder on the radio and when *Everyday People* finished he spoke to me in his tender and wise manner, reminding me of my nan.

'Nina, to stay here now would be nonsense really. I can remember when I first met you, you reminded me of a person who had no direction in life, you know? And now you've found it all.'

As he spoke, I felt like it was my nan's voice coming through his, somewhere in the distance she was approaching me. I saw her coming into the present moment in the café, joining my friends, sitting amongst us. Her invisible presence was strong, and her face became clearer in my mind until I could see her gentle brown eyes and smell the coconut soap that she used to wash her face with.

Now you know that it's all a question of interpretation, isn't it? We all have a story to tell.

Suddenly I was back at the river Ganges and my mother was throwing nan's ashes into the mighty river and I could see other people around us, washing, bathing, praying and the powerful smell of sandalwood wafted past me. Time had passed and now she looked younger to me somehow, as if the journey towards me was effortless and youthful. As if in transition, she was transformed.

'I'll have to organise this party now Nina, we'll have to plan this, darling. I want to see you off in style,' Davla said, sitting down next to me.

As she sat there with me, coaxing me into arranging the party with her, the candle on our table suddenly blew out. A thin wisp of what looked like blue smoke spiralled towards the ceiling. We both looked at it rising at the same time. And I could almost hear my nan laughing.

CHAPTER SEVENTEEN

When I arrived for Davla's party, I was taken aback by the view through the glass windows. The café was crammed with people; I could hardly have believed it was possible. A sign on the door said *closed tonight for private party*.

The tables had been moved to one side, one on top of another, with the stools beside them so that there was an open space in the centre of the floor and it was packed. There must have been at least thirty people in the café. I recognised some of Davla's friends. The café seemed to have expanded to accommodate for everyone.

When I pushed the door open, the music filtered onto the street. Davla waved frantically when she saw me. She looked stunning in a short red dress and red high heels. Gold glitter was scattered lightly across her cheekbones and her dark red lips stood out.

'You're looking gorgeous,' she shouted at me. 'I love that green dress. Here help me with the drinks will you?'

She seemed to have acquired a large number of disposable plastic cups full of wine. Wine bottles stood open all around her on the counter.

Eric walked over and stopped to pick up two of the cups, kissed me quickly and excused himself.

Women wore glittery tops and short skirts with high heels. The men were dressed in plain and coloured shirts with their hair slicked back.

I handed the drinks out and Davla turned the music down a little and the voice of the crowd seemed to rise higher than before.

I saw James enter the café with Tony and Sarah. He looked astonished at the number of people and he came over instantly to me.

'You look lovely Nina, sorry I missed you, I've come straight from my Derrida seminar. My God, who are all these people?'

I handed him a glass of wine and he stood near the open door, looking overwhelmed, until Sarah started speaking to him.

Tony looked like he had made an effort to dress up in his red shirt with thin gold stripes and black trousers.

Donna Summer's track *Hot Stuff* started and the crowd shifted. People started to dance in their limited positions and people walking past glanced in curiously.

I finished handing out the wine and took one for myself. James, Tony and Sarah came over to me.

'I hope you'll remember this, Nina,' James said, raising his cup towards me.

'This party is fantastic,' Tony said loudly. 'Don't you think so, Sarah?'

'It's not like the same place,' Sarah shouted. 'Goodness, it's too loud in here, are these all friends of yours?'

I shook my head.

'Who are all these people then?'

'Who cares? Let's enjoy their company,' Tony said. I was unused to seeing him so cheerful.

Donna Summer's voice ebbed away and Bob Marley's *could you be loved* replaced it.

As the evening progressed, Tony became bolder. James and I were surprised to see how well Sarah and him were getting on.

An hour passed and more people came and others went. The crowd became more animated and the noise became a jumble of undecipherable voices. The laughter echoed in the café and it seemed to be growing by the minute. The noise of everyone was like a rushing stream, voices upon voices, until it became a rising tide of words.

By midnight people had started leaving and eventually James and Eric put back some of the tables and stools and the music was turned down. The last remaining strangers left soon afterwards, until it was only the familiar people in the café again.

Tony and Sarah were sitting together near the window sharing a bottle of wine.

'You've hit the nail on the head there, Tony. It was a difficult time and David was only interested in himself, it was the children I felt sorry for,' I heard Sarah say.

'You need to take care of yourself,' Tony said, his voice slightly slurred.

James and Davla were talking to each other. Eric was clearing up quickly behind the counter, where the remains of the evening were scattered, bottles, cups and peanuts were strewn across the floor. He saw me looking, and observed that I was sitting alone. He threw down the black bin bag that he was throwing everything into and approached me.

'I can do that later,' he said.

The wine was unbalancing me slightly. I sat down precariously on the stool and Eric sat next to me. Davla and James were talking to each other at another table. James started laughing loudly and Davla joined in.

'James, what am I going to do with you?' she said fondly afterwards.

Eric smiled softly. 'How's the old man going to cope when you leave?'

***

'Bloody good question!' Pieter said, loudly, rudely interrupting my story. 'What did you tell Eric, that James might pine away without you?'

'You're too drunk to care,' I said and Pieter laughed.

'I'm still in control,' he said.

'Maybe you should let go,' I said. 'Let your imagination take over, once in a while.'

'Come on Nina, what happened?' Pieter asked, impatiently. 'We're close to the end, how does this tale finish?'

***

'I don't know how James will cope. I mean his flat is still a mess. It's like after his wife died, he just forgot to clear it or something,' I said to Eric.

'That's not a good indication,' Eric chuckled. 'We'll be here if he needs us.'

'He told me he could have fallen in love with me, but I was more like a daughter to him.'

'I knew that already,' Eric said and he looked around to make sure no-one was listening. 'I had that feeling he loved you. How do you feel about that, babe?'

'I'm fine with it, nothing untoward has happened.'

Eric laughed and we drank more wine. The café became like a surreal merry-go-round that was slowly starting to turn as I drank more wine.

Sarah and Tony had their heads close together.

Tony briefly looked around the café. He saw me looking in his direction and he lifted his hand and waved at me. His face looked happy and his gesture was one of confidence. I smiled at him and Sarah looked at me blankly, as if she didn't recognise me anymore.

'Do you think they're about to get married now?' Eric asked me and I laughed.

'Alcohol can do crazy things to people, maybe they were in love all along and only just realised it,' he said.

'Now they can go to all the gigs together,' I grinned and Eric almost fell off his stool laughing.

'Seriously though Nina, you know James used to come into the café really depressed in the weeks immediately after his wife had died.'

'Of course, he told me himself.'

'I just don't want him to get like that again when you leave.'

'I don't think he will but nothing is certain, of course. James is a sensitive soul,' I said.

'Listen to you. A sensitive soul, indeed, that is even if you believe in souls, now you're talking like he's converted you to believe in Jesus and all that Christian stuff.'

'I do believe in something, Eric. Call it God, call it Jesus, call it Buddha, I'm sure there is something out there now and maybe it's the very thing that we all search for,' I said.

'Yes, and a few of us find,' Eric said. 'I'm so proud of you! You've found meaning in your life long before I did in mine. So, what's the café saying to you tonight?'

***

'Don't tell me the café spoke to you now,' Pieter said. 'Was it like the voice of God?' he grinned.

'Shut up, Pieter,' I said. 'It wasn't like that, more like a merry-go-round that we were all sitting on and we were on the ride of our lives. It was the only one of its kind in the world, because it would never happen again. The ride had left our heads spinning. We held on fiercely, as we spun faster and faster. I felt as though I now understood a much bigger reality. It was as if we had to understand the interaction happening in that place because it was all for our benefit. I think the café was playing games with us that night, it was teasing us and humouring us.'

'I'm not sure I get that,' Pieter said.

'You really don't have to get it,' I said. 'I *get* it and that's what matters the most.'

Pieter stared at me.

***

James looked at me and Eric.

'You're both far too drunk,' he said.

'Look who's talking.' Eric laughed and his voice seemed to linger in the café.

I stepped outside the café at around three in the morning and the street outside was quiet. The sky was an inky black and the air was warm.

As I watched everyone inside the café through the glass, it occurred to me again, that this was a time in history that would never repeat itself. The significance of my thought flashed across my mind, like lightning striking every part of my Being.

As I saw Sarah touch Tony's arm and Davla looking tired now as she nodded at James, I knew that those movements, the touches and the conversations, would melt away into time after the night was over. It was the impermanence of the world, a constant flux, a furious river that washed our memories away with its savage waters.

I realised that it was those places, those people there at the time; that made us who we were. When we remembered later, much later, we saw a tender smile or a kind word, or even a hilarious joke and we transformed it into a time that only we understood. It became personal to us, once we had snatched it back from the river of time, from the impermanence of life.

James' arm wound around Davla, Sarah and Eric making a coffee, Tony patting his hair in the mirror, I watched it all through the glass wall, and when I touched the glass of the café it seemed to me to be alive, like a container full of wonder and life. A place where time had temporarily taken shelter to bring together all the people who were there to share their experiences and learn a little about what life was about. It was a ride that we had all taken, and now we had to get off because it had stopped.

Nobody saw me looking through the glass and I stayed there for a while, my hand warm against the coolness of the surface. When I went back in the café, the outline of my hand was still sketched on the glass, a testimony to the evening, a brief moment when time had slid into my hand.

'James, go home and get some rest. You've had far too much tonight,' Eric said.

'We should all go if that's the case,' Tony said.

'Well, folks it's been great but I'm ready to leave, shall I call a cab?' Sarah said, picking her handbag up and looking at Tony.

'No need for that, I'll walk with you. There's a mini cab office just around the corner,' Tony said. They wished me the best and the inky black outside swallowed them up, as soon as they crossed the street.

'James, you look kind of lonely. Are you thinking about Angela again?' Davla asked.

James looked at Eric and then at me, as if we held the answer to her question. He started to fiddle with the tarot cards that Davla had left on the table. He stared at the colourful cards intently, as if seeing something in the pictures that no one else could and he became lost in his thoughts.

Eric glanced at me.

'Let's go and finish clearing up,' he said to Davla gently.

'I don't feel like it right now,' Davla started to say.

'We need to finish now,' Eric said, sternly.

Davla was too drunk to say anything back. She just gave him a puzzled look. They both disappeared to the back of the café and I heard them whispering loudly.

James picked up all the cards and tried to put them all in one pile. Suddenly, he dropped them and the cards scattered on the floor like dominoes crashing down. The effect of the cards was like the thought that emerged from the caverns of the café, the one thought that James had tried to disguise during the course of the evening. His thought spilt out like the cards that lay in their brilliance on the floor.

What I wouldn't give for just another hour to be with her, when I can see her and feel her again.

'James, I know what you're thinking, I know you want to be with her.' I stood close to him.

'Am I so transparent to you, Nina?' he asked.

'I have lived with you and learnt some things.'

'I've faced her death now but it can still creep up on me.'

'Of course it can, but you're coping much better.'

Nina Simone's voice came at us from the radio, raw and distinct as ever, and James and I looked at each other and smiled.

'She's one of my favourites,' he said. 'This is a slow song, but would you like to dance?'

We pushed the table closer to the back wall with the mirrors and then we danced to Nina Simone. James held my hands and we moved slowly, our feet moving awkwardly at first. Nina Simone's edgy voice was singing about skin being black, arms being long, hair being woolly, back being strong.

James sang along, his eyes closed tightly. He swayed lightly and laughed to himself at the sound of his own voice.

But great as she was, Nina Simone was making me sad. Her deep voice resonated into the very walls of the café. A strange melancholic cry began to drift into the place. The cry was beginning to cut into me.

The song ended and another began and still James and I danced slowly together. We moved very softly to the rhythm of the song. And in those rhythms, in those lulling voices and gentle melodies, something was beginning to resurface, like tiny creatures coming out of the sand.

It began with me looking at James and suddenly feeling as if I wasn't holding James anymore, as if he were slipping from my hands. An understanding began to show itself to me that I had never been aware of before. The tiny creatures were scurrying away, as if they'd only just woken up after years of sleep, buried deep in the warm sand.

I closed my eyes and continued dancing. My body was swaying in time to the slow music from side to side, when it seemed that everything before me began to pass away. The stools, the tables, the mirrors, the counter, the bookshelves, the lights, everything became blurry and then vanished altogether, as if time had finally caught up with it, and carried it all away in a bundle on its whirlwind back.

Everything that I knew, that was familiar in the environment was being stripped away. It was all simply disappearing, layer by layer, material by material, until all that was left was me.

It was me, and what I was composed of. It was the rhythm of my body, the rhythm that is constant in each of us, that keeps us alive every day. I felt the blood pounding inside me, I knew every muscle and I felt every nerve, and the pumping of my heart, I could feel the acute beat that worked inside me.

Finally, I felt the silence that was there, the silence that lived in all its profundity in every human being. Beyond that silence was profound peace that was the core of me. Peace that I had found through the café. The café that was disappearing before my very eyes, vanishing into the unknown. It was the mystery of the vanishing café, I found myself wondering if it had ever existed at all.

I opened my eyes to James' prompting; he was touching my arm and saying something.

'Are you enjoying the music?' His eyes were shining with happiness.

The café was charged as if an electric current had just struck it, a yellow glow bathed everything; it was all I could see, apart from James.

As I watched James, I saw him talking and I saw his lips moving, but I couldn't hear the words coming out of his mouth. The yellow light in the café moved over to the top of James' head, and it hung there precariously, as if it were about to drop on him at any second. It entered his mouth and he appeared to swallow it. Suddenly, it was as if I was seeing right through James, through his skin and heart and personality, to his soul, to his very *essence.* I was seeing who he really was.

What is James made of? I thought.

He continued to talk to me, he even laughed. I was looking at him, but really I was looking *beyond* him. It was like I was *really* seeing him for the first time since I'd known him.

Then it was all gone. The stools and tables defined themselves again, the bookshelves reappeared; the tarot cards were messy on the floor. The world was returning, the glass wall of the café was visible again. The music was louder than I remembered. My head was pounding. I was feeling giddy and James was gripping my arm and asking me if I was okay.

I didn't respond to him immediately and he let go of me and disappeared towards the counter and then around the back to where Eric and Davla were. I was left standing alone in the middle of the floor. I sat down on a stool near the back of the café.

***

Pieter was speechless for a few minutes and I thought maybe the drink had finally got to him. Eventually, he spoke up.

'The café vanished before you, right? You're telling me that the café simply evaporated that night. It just disappeared to God knows where, honestly? How the hell is that possible, please tell me.' He was pleading with me now.

'Pieter, trust me, it did vanish. I don't know how, it defied all the laws we know about, it just did. Just accept it.'

Pieter gulped the whole glass of wine down in one go and I laughed.

***

In the café, James came back with a glass of water.

'What's wrong with you?' he asked me.

'I'm feeling sick,' I said and he gave me a knowing look.

'You really are such a lightweight, my dear. If you can't handle your drink, it's best to stick to the coke.'

I couldn't really fathom what was happening, but the café was revealing itself in yet another different way than before. The place was quiet now, as if all the surprises had been sprung for the night.

'What a brilliant night, but I think I'm getting a bit too old for these late night parties,' James said. 'There you go, dear, are you feeling better now?'

It was almost four in the morning when we all had a round of coffee. We drank quietly, as if we were sitting facing each other in a transforming ritual, with the glass windows separating us from the world outside. If anyone had walked past the café during the time that we sat there, they must have thought it strange that a group of people were sitting around a table in the depths of early morning, looking like they were holding a lonely vigil.

James sighed contentedly as he drank his coffee; his fingers wrapped thickly around the cup.

If I let go, what will happen? Will I be floating in a wilderness that I don't understand? What will happen to me then?

His voice was a gentle plea, a silent prayer that emanated from him and disappeared like soft smoke into the walls of the café.

James and I left later. I was still feeling the effects of the wine, but James seemed to have sobered up considerably. He joked about Sarah and Tony and their newfound respect for each other on the way home.

I didn't answer him and he took that as a sign that I was listening, so he chattered on mindlessly. He was in a boisterous mood now, oblivious to the fact that I wasn't paying much attention. His soft chuckles added a sense of comfort to our walk and the sound of his voice was like an invisible path that spread out before us until we reached home.

EPILOGUE

Five years passed before I fully appreciated the impact that the café had made on my life. Those five years were filled with getting to understand my role in my new job, having a wonderful social life and a new husband.

It was thrilling for me to move to an unfamiliar city and to grow to love it. Amsterdam was the place that encouraged me to reach the dizzying heights of success in my work and in my marriage.

'I know all that already Nina, but how does this story end?' Pieter asked. 'Do I continue sitting here near the café, hearing how it disappeared and then go back to the hotel? We built a wall between us today. Do we keep it there or move it away?'

'I don't know, your scepticism of my story concerns me, of course it does. You liked the unpolished diamond that you found in me, but now that I've come clean, you seem to be throwing me away, our marriage away.'

'Our beliefs are so different, that's clear now,' Pieter said. 'We have a lot of talking to do back in Amsterdam. Until then, you must finish what you started.'

His words saddened me and I remembered that I hadn't kept in contact with James after I'd left London, even though I had told him I would. I had lost my precious contact book and with it a host of media contacts and the details of Davla, Sarah and Eric. I cursed myself a hundred times in Amsterdam when I needed it and I wrote to James only nine months after being in Holland. He never replied and I thought perhaps he was disappointed with me.

I reasoned that in my hurry to leave London, I must have left my contact book at James' place, he was probably holding it for me, turning it over in his hands, his weathered fingers opening the pages, waiting for me to contact him so that he could send it to me.

'If he had your contact book he surely would have called you,' Pieter said, as if he were reading my thoughts.

'I was too busy, as I had started my job working as a Press Officer under Mr Klute's direction with a team that helped to promote educational projects in third world countries. I wrote endless press releases about our work in Brazil, Africa and India and worked on campaigns to promote exhibitions held locally. My work involved targeting young children and single mothers. As you know, I became successful and made a name for myself in the organisation. At the end of two years, I was promoted to a more senior role and I sometimes had to travel internationally.'

There was no time to dwell on anything other than my work and adjusting to life in another country.

'It was only after the death of your mother Pieter, just after we moved in together towards the end of the third year, that I remembered the café again. I wish I could see James again, if only for old time's sake, he was special,' I said.

'Special?' Pieter scoffed. 'Nina, you've ignored him for a long time, why remember him now?' he asked.

'I was busy getting on with life, but I never forgot him,' I said.

Pieter looked across the road at the desolate café.

'No one knows where he is now, isn't that enough?' he said.

I suppose the café had to be put in its rightful place in history, the way events often do after they have occurred, like a book that has been read and is waiting to be stacked in a library with a host of others.

I recalled that hot summer again and there were images that stood out in my mind. Davla's yellow stilettos, the books piled up in James' living room. Casting my mind back further, Sarah writing letters to her children, only to screw them up and start again, Eric with a tea towel over his shoulder. It was like a circle that had no beginning and no end.

'Isn't Eric supposed to be here by now?' Pieter asked, glancing at his watch.

We waited another ten minutes and then I saw Eric and with him was Davla. Eric looked the same except that his dreads were shorter, he wore jeans and a simple cream jacket and he looked more elegant than I remembered him. Davla looked more sophisticated too, she had dyed her hair a lighter shade of brown and it was cut shorter, just over her shoulders. She looked tanned and only had a touch of pink lip-gloss which made her look younger.

'Eric!' I shouted and they both turned around. 'What a surprise, you've both come.'

Davla smiled. I stood up and Eric came over and hugged me tightly.

'Babe, it's really you!' he said, smiling broadly. 'You're a naughty one, leaving and forgetting about us just like that.'

They sat down and I introduced them to Pieter.

'So, you're the famous Pieter, it's good to meet you,' Eric said, smiling warmly.

'I've been hearing all about this café, it's got quite a reputation,' Pieter said.

Davla affectionately patted my arm and asked me how I was.

'You must be wondering why the café is closed. Jesus, it seems so long ago now,' she said.

'I need to know what's happened. I mean, this is tragic.'

Davla and Eric both looked at each other as if they didn't know where to begin. Then they started to speak at the same time.

The waitress came over and Pieter bought a round for everyone.

'We gave you all our contact details and you must have been busy but we never heard anything,' Eric said.

'Sorry, my life took off, I changed everything including my phone numbers.'

They looked at each other again, searching each other's faces.

'When did you close the café?' I asked Davla.

'Recently, about six months ago, it was a long process.'

'What happened?'

'As everyone knows, I wasn't happy there. You can probably remember that things weren't great with my mother. I had a long chat with my dad about it and told him that I was thinking of going to Brazil and teaching English. Nina, it was the best thing I could have done. Naturally, he was upset at first but he gradually accepted my decision.'

'She put the café up for sale early last year and promptly left for Sao Paulo, leaving her father to deal with agents and prospective buyers. I miss that place,' Eric said.

'I think there is an interested party coming next week to see it,' Davla said.

'So you're back in Brazil now?' I asked.

'Yes, I'm staying with my cousin in Sao Paulo, a mile from the district where I grew up and I'm working part-time in a jewellery store and training to be a teacher. You're lucky you caught me actually, I thought I'd come with Eric, I'm visiting the family here but I'm going back next week.'

'You look so well, Nina. You must be living life to the full over there,' Eric said. He looked at my wedding ring briefly and his eyes searched my face.

They listened eagerly as I quickly told them about life in Amsterdam over the past five years and my success in my job.

'I always knew you'd do well, I had no worries about you at all,' Eric smiled.

'What about the others? How is James, do you still see him?' I asked.

Eric took a sharp intake of breath and let it out suddenly.

'Actually, that's why I was trying to reach you for such a long time, babe.' He looked across at Davla but she was waiting for him to speak. The atmosphere became cold and a feeling of dread entered me. Even before he told me, I knew what he was going to say.

'I'm sorry Nina, but James died,' Eric said and his voice was barely a whisper, like a leaf caught in a breeze.

The air was pregnant with his affirmation and a terrible feeling came upon me.

'James died?' I echoed, and I felt a sudden tightening in my chest.

Pieter leaned in closer in his chair.

'How, *when?*' I asked and my voice sounded like it belonged to someone else.

He told me then, everything that had happened. His story unfolded slowly, as if he were reading from a book and taking his time turning the pages.

'After you left, James still came to the café, although it was far less. He rarely talked to anyone when he arrived.'

'We gave up on him after a while,' Davla interrupted. 'He didn't want to talk to us, so we left him to read his paper or his books in peace.'

'It wasn't that he was depressed, more thoughtful. We knew he didn't want to talk much, so we didn't push it. After a few months, we thought we'd try again. We waited until the last customer left one evening and then approached him as he sat reading a book,' Eric continued.

'We were all planning a trip to the theatre on Saturday and we asked James if he wanted to come. He said that his sister was coming down to stay from Dublin the next day, so we invited her along and he cheered up a bit after that.'

'He was in a funny way that night and it had me worried. He was talking about his wife again, mentioning their trips together and he had a cold, I remember that because it was freezing outside. It was typical February weather and I made him a hot chocolate to warm him up. We sat there until two in the morning, just me and him,' Eric said.

'Nina, he really missed you. He said your company had been good for him, we joked that you must have had an affair,' Davla said.

Pieter looked at her sharply but she did not notice him staring.

'He asked me to come back and see him,' I said, my throat felt like sandpaper. I took a sip of my drink.

Eric told me everything, as if he were reading James' story, page by page.

'We kept trying to contact you because we thought maybe he'd feel better if he heard from you. No one could remember the company you were working for, we got it mixed up with another organisation, it was a nightmare.'

'I'm so sorry,' I said and Eric smiled sadly.

Davla was looking over at the café across the road. It seemed darker than ever.

'We agreed to meet James with the others outside the theatre with his sister,' Davla said. 'He was taking her around London, showing her all the museums and art galleries. He was even joking again, we thought everything was fine.'

'Anyway, they didn't show up at the theatre and everyone was annoyed. He didn't answer his mobile either, so we thought he had changed his mind. None of us knew the truth,' Eric continued.

'How did you find out?' I asked.

'Two days went past and then his sister came to the café with her husband and I was the only one there. As soon as I saw her, I knew something was wrong, it was written all over her face. She told us that James had died in his sleep the night before the show and apparently it was a heart attack. We were stunned. She said that she didn't know us, but she felt that she had to let us know. That was a really strange, really terrible day,' Eric said.

He stared into his drink as if he couldn't bear to look at me. I felt a lump in my throat and tears sting my eyes. Pieter watched me now and his lack of affection bothered me greatly. He did not offer his hand to me or any comfort at all.

'I should have stayed in touch, it's so stupid,' I said.

'There was nothing you could have done,' Eric said, matter-of-factly. 'His sister, Cara, that was her name – waited for him to wake up in the morning, they had planned to visit an art gallery that day. After a while she became concerned and knocked on his door.'

'He died peacefully, Nina,' Davla said.

'How can you know that?' I asked, a little sharply.

'We only know what Cara told us. She said his expression was serene and he looked like he was only sleeping. It must have been during the night, the exact time she couldn't be sure. She phoned the hospital and her husband immediately. He came down the same day.'

'James was buried in a cemetery in South London, next to his wife. It was near the school where he used to teach, we've visited a couple of times. Davla closed the café for the morning, and everyone went to the funeral service, Tony and Sarah, it was beautiful. His sister read poetry by Yeats and psalm 23 about walking through the valley of the shadow of death. She had us all in tears,' Eric said.

I felt as if I had been shaken to my very core.

'I should have been there.' I said.

'You weren't to know,' Pieter said and Eric looked at him and then at me and nodded slowly.

'I'm sorry we had to tell you today,' he said, softly.

I felt tears threaten to overflow and I fumbled for the napkin.

Eric pulled his chair closer and put his hand on my arm. We sat there quietly for a long time remembering James and talking about our memories of him.

'Sometimes he really used to wind me up,' Davla said laughing. 'He was so set in his ways, but Nina, he changed after he met you. I think he must have really liked you.'

'What makes you say that?'

'He just spoke about you in positive ways, I mean he compared you to his wife. That made us all suspicious!'

'He did?' I asked.

'He said Angela had waltzed into his life one day and you did the same, like a butterfly, I believe he said!' Eric said.

'We really thought you guys had something going on,' Davla smiled.

'No, we didn't,' I said and Pieter glanced at me. 'We *really* didn't.'

'I suppose sometimes people just click, as if you've known them for years,' Eric said, looking at Pieter.

A short while later Davla left us. She gave me her contact details and told me to stay in contact, but I knew that I would never see her again. She had changed a lot; that much was certain. It was clear that she had built a new life for herself in Brazil. I knew that the café was never as special to her as it had been to me and Eric.

The café had made me feel as if it were a special place, where the vast ocean of life was always playing a small part. I couldn't help but stare at it again across the road and it was as if that ocean had dried up now into a desert.

The evening grew darker and we ordered more drinks. I wanted to speak to Eric alone and as if he were reading my mind, Pieter spoke up.

'Perhaps I'll leave you two to catch up,' he said, a little later. 'I've heard a lot today and there's a hell of a lot to think about.' He smiled wryly and then took me aside as he paid the bill. I noticed he was slightly unsteady on his feet. I could feel Eric watching us.

Pieter was cold in the way he spoke to me. His indifference was shocking. I felt my heart close up. I guarded the love that I had for him. I could not believe that my marriage might all be over in a day of intense story telling. It was as if love was the last thing on Pieter's mind. James, a man who was now dead, was firmly etched in his thoughts, like a shadowy ghost, that had been plaguing him for a long time.

'Nina, we have to talk once we get home,' he said, in a matter-of-fact way. 'It seems like we need to find each other again.'

'Pieter, this is my story of how I found you, don't you get it? It's ironic that since telling you about the café, you've lost me somehow.'

'I'm tired and I need to think this over, I don't know what this means for us right now. My mind is in turmoil. I just find it hard to believe all the magic in this. Maybe you married a boring, rationalist after all.'

'Maybe I did,' I said, sadly.

'This is all new for me: life after death and all that hocus pocus in the café. I just don't know what's real right now,' Pieter said, placing his credit card back into his wallet.

I felt panic rush through me, but I remained calm as he looked at me, his eyes searching mine for an answer.

'Pieter, it's me, the woman you fell in love with. This is a part of me that I didn't show you before and now I feel like you're punishing me for it.'

'Nina, stay with your friend now and let's see what decision we make back in Amsterdam,' Pieter said.

'What are you saying?' I asked. 'Are you dumping me because I believe in life after death?'

'Nina, I'm not dumping you.' He looked exasperated. 'We just need to talk,' he said wearily, unsteady again on his feet.

'You're not as reliable as I thought, Pieter. If you don't accept me for who I am, this marriage is over.' I stood my ground and I left him standing there, holding his wallet, looking forlornly at the desolate café one last time, before leaving Soho.

'What's wrong?' Eric asked me as I tearfully returned to him.

'I think my marriage may be finished,' I said and I started crying.

'Are you joking?' Eric asked.

'No, I told Pieter the story of the café from afternoon until now, we've been sitting here and all its done is exposed the cracks in our marriage.'

'What happened? I did notice he was tense when you spoke about James.'

'He thinks James and I were lovers,' I said and Eric laughed.

'You're kidding!' Eric said. 'That was the past, why do people choose to live in the past?'

'It's easier than facing your fears now,' I said. 'Pieter was tense with just about everything in my story. Eric, you know that place was special, that the energy in there was Godlike, for want of a better word. You know I saw my nan in there and James' wife. Well, it turns out that Pieter doesn't believe in life after death. He won't even contemplate it. It's ridiculous. He thought I was too grief stricken and I was hallucinating and made everything up. Eric, he thinks I'm mad, my own husband, doesn't believe me.'

'Whoa, that *must* have been some afternoon,' Eric said. 'A bit like a war unfolding. He's had too much to drink, maybe tomorrow you can sort it out.'

'He wants to talk back in Amsterdam, God only knows what that will bring.'

Eric sighed. 'I hope for your sake, it's not that bad, eh?' He came over to me and hugged me warmly. 'What a shame that some people are so closed to life after death.'

'I feel like by sitting close to the café, I can remember James again,' I said to Eric.

'I've got something to give you actually,' Eric said and he took a book out of his rucksack. 'You left it at James' flat and he asked me to give it to you. He thought you would come back to the café.'

A mixture of emotions rose in me and fell away again, like waves coming to the shore and then retreating. I took my contact book from him and saw all their names and details written near the back. I imagined James' hands on the cover of my book, desperately trying to find a number for me. There was a tragic irony to it all. So, that was it. The café was closed forever with the passing away of James.

Eric sat patiently with me for quite a while.

Nan's voice pulled at me fiercely, tugging at me like a kite I was struggling to hold onto in the wind. She was talking about faces and people, about the strangers who passed me on my journeys. The way they walked, the tales they told. There were so many stories upon stories, so many layers.

I glanced at Eric and he was watching me, a soft smile playing on his lips.

Look at the hands, look at the way people walk; it's never the same. See if the expression on their faces is pain or indifference; learn to read people like a book.

I felt my voice tremble slightly as I asked the waiter for a glass of water. The air was cooler than before and I felt cold.

James is dead, I told myself and my mind protested my thought.

No, he's not! The man's alive; he's sitting at home reading Dostoevsky by candlelight, he's eating with Sarah somewhere in China town, he's dancing like a madman to Nina Simone.

I thought of him and in a single flash his face came into my mind, then just as quickly, it faded away like smoke vanishing into the air.

The moment of death is the moment of truth.

His words echoed in me, as if he'd just whispered them in my ears.

I felt as if a feather had brushed my left ear and I instinctively touched it, thinking that an insect had flown past. I drank my water quickly.

Eric slipped his hand in mine as we left the bar and walked over to the other side of the street. He told me to look at the café once more and I replied that it was shrouded in darkness.

'Don't you believe it's still a magical place?' he asked and his voice made me curious.

We came close to the glass, but there was nothing to see inside. It reminded me of a wreckage of a ship under the ocean. There were clues to its inhabitants like articles strewn on the seabed. I saw the outline of a book, and a spoon, but that was it. The café was not friendly to me, it was the ghost of the place it once was. Its stillness infuriated me and I wanted to throw something at the place. I wanted it to remember me and acknowledge the life that it had once in it.

It was strange then, I felt something prod me on my shoulder.

There was no one behind us, only a slight shift in the air.

We stood on the edge of the curb facing the café door. It seemed that a pinprick of light was visible on the surface of the glass door in the middle. When I looked back, the pinprick had grown and it was getting bigger by the second. Soon it was the size of a football. Whatever it was, it had tremendous energy and the light was almost blinding us. Eric's hand broke free from mine as he shielded his eyes.

The light surged forward with an almighty force; it was like a swirling tunnel. We stepped back quickly, so that we were off the curb and on the street.

'Jesus, something's happening!' I said excitedly and Eric laughed at my astonishment.

'You didn't think I'd let you go home like this, did you babe?' He asked. 'Let's see what the café has in store for us.'

The ball of light was huge and the colour was a pure blinding white. It was like a cleansing fire, I'd never seen anything like it. The door was soon engulfed in tremendous white flames; they lapped at the sides and soon immersed it with their strength. The door vanished within the white flames. They swallowed it up.

After a moment the light dimmed and we saw a figure standing in the doorway. A figure whose image seemed to be slightly blurred around the edges; the contours of the body were not clear. Yet it was unmistakable that it was James.

His clothes were the same, the navy blazer and the corduroy trousers. His body seemed illumined; it was as if a torch was shining *through* him. He looked up, and he seemed to be looking sideways, but it was really at us. It was as if his sense of perception was different to ours, yet he knew that we were in his presence.

He had a hat on and an ethereal quality around him; it enveloped him like a huge coat. Warmth emanated from him, a feeling of peace that took over my freezing hands and cold body. The sadness that I remembered clinging to him wasn't present anymore.

I wasn't sure but he appeared to smile. He moved his arms up, as if he wanted to show us something that he was holding. No words came from him, no words were necessary. Suddenly, I knew what he wanted us to know.

It was his wife, he felt her again. I knew that he was with her, their faces close, their breath becoming one. He touched the curve of her back as she lay beside him, he kissed her forehead and wept that he had found her again.

There is magic in life, there is sadness and love; there is something that never dies.

His words rang through us, but he didn't say them, he conveyed them as he stood there.

She laid her head on his chest, and he whispered her name. She took his hand and wrapped hers in it. They were intertwined together, skin upon skin, breath upon breath; two figures that merged into one and that became the essence of one person. His hands were smooth as they held her tightly.

In life there's suffering, in death there's peace. The pain that runs deep in life like a thunderous river becomes the tree under which we rest when we pass over.

When he touched her face and looked in her eyes, he recognized what he saw. The familiarity of it swept over him, as if throughout eternity it was the one image that stayed still, untainted by the passing of time.

The light from the door highlighted James' face. It distorted his features, its tremendous current like electricity flickered over him. The energy from the light was overpowering for me, I wanted to step further into the street, but I was transfixed. I stayed still, fearing that the image would fade if I moved.

James moved his arm up and suddenly took his hat off. We watched, amazed as thousands of small balls of light came out of his hat. They started to drift upwards like transparent bubbles. I looked closer, and realised that they weren't balls of light at all; they were butterflies, hundreds of them. He had released a stream of them; they had flowed out of his hat like magic.

I wanted to laugh out loud. James, my friend, the philosopher had transformed. He was a magician now, the tricks that had fallen upon him in life, he had defeated in death.

The butterflies were magnificent and beautiful. They were different colours, not possible in the physical realm, shimmering silvers, iridescent pink, shiny brown, some even changed colours the higher they flew. I wanted to capture them, keep them as my testimony, but I knew that it wouldn't be possible. The butterflies kept emerging from James' hat and they travelled upwards and seemed to vanish into the thin air, somewhere near the top of the café, where the canopy used to be. A particularly pretty one caught my eye. The body was silver, the wings tipped with intense yellow and red, like the sun spreading itself over the first break of dawn.

In the blink of an eye, the figure of James started to fade. He still held his hat and the butterflies still came forth, although it seemed less than before.

He was telling us something again and his words struck me with an unusual velocity.

Memory is the one thing that you can hold. Make it truly yours; mould it like a potter shaping his clay. Nothing lasts forever; impermanence is the nature of life. Memory is the key to holding what you cherish the most.

His words slowed, they faded with the flames. The light began to dim as the flames subsided. The butterflies were vanishing as suddenly as they had appeared. The blurred edges quickly cleared so that the shape of the door came through the dying embers of the white flames again. It was coming into focus once more, the darkness within taking over the subsiding light. James' figure appeared to be stepping into the light; he seemed to be walking away from us. The dimness in the café returned and soon the furthest end was black again.

James' figure, still holding the hat, became a tiny blot on the glass door. The pinprick of light was swallowed up, like a whirling wind. Yet it seemed to me that his presence still lingered before us, in the space in front of my eyes.

As the door returned to normal and the darkness became apparent again within, James' words burned in my mind.

'Pieter is not going to believe this,' I shouted. 'He should be here now to see this for himself,' I said to Eric.

'That is a shame indeed,' Eric said. I felt sadness at his words but elation at seeing James.

'What if Pieter tells me tomorrow that I'm crazy and he wants a logical wife, who can bring up his kids and never feel with her heart or experience anything like this magic? Oh my God Eric, it's scary how quickly it might all crumble.'

Eric hugged me.

'Be yourself, Nina. Follow the truth you've always known, the seed that your grandma planted. No matter what happens, you can't diminish the experience that the café gave you. It may vanish, as everything vanishes in time, but it firmly stays rooted in your heart and that will never go,' he said.

Eric stood on the pavement, watching me tenderly. My marriage fears subsided for a moment as I looked at the café again.

There was undoubtedly still something powerful about the place, a voice that it spoke with to summon up the memories of the past. James' image stubbornly refused to disappear; it hovered in the place like a strange insect. I could still see James holding his hat, carrying away the magnificent secrets of the café with him.

Eric and I held hands and silently watched the café. We both knew what the café was capable of and yet it had surprised us yet again with its magic in showing us that James was happy.

To others walking past, the café seemed like a neglected place again and the street assumed nothing had happened. We continued standing there for a while, the force of the vision still fresh before us, until eventually we left.

Before I returned to the hotel to face my drunk husband, I wished the café would suddenly reappear in all its glory tomorrow morning, so that I could show Pieter again, before we flew back to Amsterdam. He would see its power and I would win back his trust.

Instead, darkness came over the café swiftly and it made James' image fade into it, until what was left of him was only a shadow, a vanishing memory, a fingerprint embedded deeply in its walls.

Printed in Great Britain
by Amazon

32639047R00111